200 HARLEY STREET

Welcome to the luxurious premises of
the exclusive Hunter Clinic, world renowned
in plastic and reconstructive surgery,
set right on Harley Street, the centre of
elite clinical excellence, in the heart of
London's glittering West End!

Owned by two very different brothers,
Leo and Ethan Hunter, the Hunter Clinic
undertakes both cosmetic and reconstructive
surgery. Playboy Leo handles the rich and
famous clients, enjoying the red carpet
glamour of London's A-list social scene,
while brooding ex-army doc Ethan
focuses his time on his passion—
transforming the lives of injured war heroes
and civilian casualties of war.

Emotion and drama abound against the
backdrop of one of Europe's most glamorous
cities, as Leo and Ethan work
through their tensions and find women
who will change their lives for ever!

200 HARLEY STREET

*Glamour, intensity, desire—the lives and loves
of London's hottest team of surgeons!*

Dear Reader

London holds a very special place in my heart. I had my first year of schooling there and I lived in Prince Albert Road, so close to the zoo I could often hear the animals at night. It's always a treat to revisit London, either in person or through the characters in my stories and this one—Rafael and Abbie's story—has been a joy.

I have two passionate people bound together by their baby daughter, but then pushed too far apart by the unbearably tough times they have to go through.

Do you have a mantra that pops up during tough times? I've been known to use 'no pain, no gain' or 'what doesn't kill you makes you stronger'. I'm not so sure about 'the end justifies the means', or 'you have to break eggs to make an omelette', because the significance of what is lost or broken might not be apparent until it's too late to realise how important it was.

All too often what gets broken is a relationship that couldn't survive the pain. Repairing that kind of damage to love needs a bit of magic, I think. And what better place to find magic like that than in one of my favourite cities?

Happy reading :)

With love,

Alison

200 HARLEY STREET: THE PROUD ITALIAN

BY
ALISON ROBERTS

MILLS
BOON

First published in Great Britain 2014
by Mills & Boon, an imprint of Harlequin (UK) Limited,
Large Print edition 2014
Eton House, 18-24 Paradise Road,
Richmond, Surrey, TW9 1SR

© 2014 Harlequin Books S.A.

Special thanks and acknowledgement are given to Alison Roberts for her contribution to the *200 Harley Street* series

ISBN: 978-0-263-23908-9

Printed and bound in Great Britain
by CPI Antony Rowe, Chippenham, Wiltshire

Alison Roberts lives in Christchurch, New Zealand, and has written over sixty Mills & Boon® Medical Romances™.

As a qualified paramedic, she has personal experience of the drama and emotion to be found in the world of medical professionals, and loves to weave stories with this rich background—especially when they can have a happy ending.

When Alison is not writing, you'll find her indulging her passion for dancing or spending time with her friends (including Molly the dog) and her daughter Becky, who has grown up to become a brilliant artist. She also loves to travel, hates housework, and considers it a triumph when the flowers outnumber the weeds in her garden.

Recent titles by Alison Roberts:

FROM VENICE WITH LOVE‡
ALWAYS THE HERO††
NYC ANGELS: AN EXPLOSIVE REUNION~
ST PIRAN'S: THE WEDDING!†
MAYBE THIS CHRISTMAS…?
THE LEGENDARY PLAYBOY SURGEON**
FALLING FOR HER IMPOSSIBLE BOSS**
SYDNEY HARBOUR HOSPITAL: ZOE'S BABY*
THE HONOURABLE MAVERICK

‡*The Christmas Express!*
**Sydney Harbour Hospital*
†*St Piran's Hospital*
***Heartbreakers of St Patrick's Hospital*
~*NYC Angels*
††*Earthquake!*

Did you know that THE HONOURABLE MAVERICK won a 2011 *RT Book Reviews* Reviewers' Choice Award?

200 HARLEY STREET

Glamour, intensity, desire—the lives and loves of
London's hottest team of surgeons!

For the next four months enter the world of London's
elite surgeons as they transform the lives of their patients
and find love amidst a sea of passions and tensions…!

Renowned plastic surgeon and legendary playboy
Leo Hunter can't resist the challenge of unbuttoning
the intriguing new head nurse, Lizzie Birch!
200 HARLEY STREET: SURGEON IN A TUX
by Carol Marinelli

Glamorous Head of PR Lexi Robbins is determined
to make gruff, grieving and super-sexy Scottish surgeon Iain MacKenzie
her Hunter Clinic star!
200 HARLEY STREET: GIRL FROM THE RED CARPET
by Scarlet Wilson

Top-notch surgeons and estranged spouses
Rafael and Abbie de Luca find being forced to work together again
tough as their passion is as incendiary as ever!
200 HARLEY STREET: THE PROUD ITALIAN
by Alison Roberts

One night with his new colleague, surgeon Grace Turner, sees
former Hollywood plastic surgeon Mitchell Cooper daring to live again…
200 HARLEY STREET: AMERICAN SURGEON IN LONDON
by Lynne Marshall

Injured war hero Prince Marco meets physical therapist
Becca Anderson—the woman he once shared a magical *forbidden*
summer romance with long ago…
200 HARLEY STREET: THE SOLDIER PRINCE
by Kate Hardy

When genius micro-surgeon Edward North meets single mum
Nurse Charlotte King she opens his eyes to a whole new world…
200 HARLEY STREET: THE ENIGMATIC SURGEON
by Annie Claydon

Junior surgeon Kara must work with hot-shot
Irish surgeon Declan Underwood—the man she kissed at the hospital ball!
200 HARLEY STREET: THE SHAMELESS MAVERICK
by Louisa George

Brilliant charity surgeon Olivia Fairchild faces the man who once
broke her heart—damaged ex-soldier Ethan Hunter. Yet she's unprepared
for his haunted eyes and the shock of his sensual touch…!
200 HARLEY STREET: THE TORTURED HERO by Amy Andrews

Experience glamour, tension, heartbreak and emotion
at 200 HARLEY STREET
in this new eight-book continuity
from Mills & Boon® Medical Romance™

These books are also available in eBook format
and in two 200 HARLEY STREET collection bundles
from www.millsandboon.co.uk

CHAPTER ONE

WINNING WAS SUPPOSED to be what mattered.

And it was. The end justified the means, didn't it?

Of course it did. That couldn't be doubted for a heartbeat in this case. The blanket-wrapped bundle in Abbie de Luca's arms was the absolute proof of that. The battle had been hard fought and gruelling enough to have almost destroyed her but she had won.

No. *Ella* had won. Her precious baby, only just a year old, had fought the killer disease of acute lymphoblastic leukaemia at an age where the greatest challenge should have been learning to sit up and take her first steps. The fact that they were being sent back from the only place in the world that had offered the new and radical treatment so that Ella could continue her recuperation at the Lighthouse Children's Hospital in London was proof of having won the battle. It meant she was a huge step closer to going home.

But was the 'home' they'd left behind still there?

For either of them?

Being escorted off the flight from New York before any other passengers and fast-tracked through customs at Heathrow airport like royalty should be making the triumph of winning all the sweeter.

So why did Abbie feel as if she was stepping onto a new battlefield? One that was only marginally less significant than the life-and-death struggle that had represented most of the three months she had been away with her tiny daughter.

'There's an ambulance waiting for you, Mrs de Luca.' The customs official eyed the wheelchair beside Abbie that the steward from the plane had been pushing. 'Is this all going with you?'

'No. It's going back on the next flight.' Abbie unwrapped Ella just enough to unhook the electrodes from the monitoring equipment. 'It was only a precaution. We didn't even need the oxygen.' They hadn't needed a medical escort either. One of the rare positive aspects of having a paediatric surgeon for a mother, although the negative side of knowing too much had outweighed that far too many times already.

Ella stirred in her arms but didn't wake. Abbie took a moment to check the connections of the central line the baby still had under her collarbone and made sure the syringe driver attached to the tubing hadn't run out of the drugs that were still a necessary part of treatment. Then she tucked it securely back into the folds of blanket and gave Ella a kiss on the few stray wisps of hair she had somehow retained.

As Ella relaxed back into sleep a tiny hand came up to touch her mother's cheek, as if she was reassuring herself that she was safe. She was probably smiling, Abbie thought, watching the crinkle deepen around the tightly closed eyes. Shame nobody could see it because of the mask needed to protect the baby from airborne infections.

The gesture had been enough to melt hearts around her anyway.

'Aww…' The burly customs official was smiling. 'What a wee pet.'

'Adorable…' The steward was blinking hard. 'I'm so happy she's going to be all right now, Abbie.'

'Thanks, Damien.' Abbie had to swallow the big lump in her own throat. Happy didn't touch the sides of how she felt about her daughter's new prognosis. 'And thanks so much for taking such good care of us on the flight.'

'It was a privilege. Have you got someone meeting you now?'

Abbie nodded. 'The ambulance is here. They're taking us to the Lighthouse. That's the children's hospital I work at.'

But the steward was shaking his head. Frowning. 'No… I meant… You know…'

Abbie did know. He meant someone with a personal attachment. Like Ella's father?

'Maybe. It was a bit of a last-minute rush and we weren't sure we'd get onto this flight. The New York team obviously managed to arrange the transfer but I'm not sure who else knows about it.'

She'd tried to ring Rafael but his phone had gone to his message service. Mr de Luca was in surgery all day, she'd been informed. Could they take a message? No, Abbie had responded. She'd be seeing him soon enough.

Or maybe that should be too soon? She'd walked out on her marriage to fight this battle. Maybe that was why success wasn't tasting as sweet as it should.

Maybe the price had been too high.

'Abbie…' The man who'd been allowed into this private area of the customs hall and was now striding towards them wasn't an airport official.

'Oh, my…' Damien clearly appreciated the attributes of the tall, sexy newcomer. 'Is that Ella's daddy?'

'No.' Abbie shook her head, bemused. 'He's more like my boss.' And clearly a commanding enough presence, even out of a medical environment, to have had rules broken for him.

The steward was grinning as he started to manoeuvre the wheelchair out of the way. 'Tough job,' he murmured, 'but I guess someone's gotta do it.'

Abbie felt her lips curve as she raised her voice. 'Ethan…what on earth are you doing here?'

'I happened to field a call to Rafael about your arrival time and the ambulance transfer. He's caught up in Theatre so I thought I'd come for the ride and make sure you had a welcoming committee.'

And who could be more appropriate than one of the Hunter brothers, the owners of the prestigious London plastic-and-reconstructive-surgery clinic that employed both of Ella's parents as specialist paediatric surgeons. The clinic that had made it financially possible for Ella to go to the States and undertake the risky, experimental treatment that had been her only hope of a cure.

'Does…does Rafael know we've come home?'

'Not yet.' Ethan's gaze gave nothing away. 'The case he's operating on today is putting him under considerable pressure. I…didn't want to distract him.' The hint of a smile was sympathetic. 'I'll let him know the moment he comes out, I promise.'

Abbie simply nodded. There was a subtext here. That Rafael would need prior warning before seeing her again? Hearing her voice, even, given that their minimal communication of late had been via text and email? That, without some kind of intermediary, his Italian pride might be enough for him to refuse to see her at all? Maybe their first meeting would involve a solicitor and official documents outlining shared custody agreements for their child. How sad would that be?

'You're good to go.' The customs official stamped their passports and nodded towards someone near the door. 'Mr Hunter shouldn't really be in here. They'll show you out to where the ambulance crew is waiting. Your luggage will be sent by taxi as soon as it's offloaded.'

Ethan picked up the cabin bag by Abbie's feet but his gaze rested on the bundle in her arms. 'You okay? Would you rather I carried Ella?'

Abbie shook her head. 'I'm good.'

She wasn't about to hand her baby to someone else to carry, despite her precious burden feeling heavier by the minute. She was exhausted, that was all. These last few months had taken their toll, physically as well as emotionally, but she couldn't afford to stop being strong.

Not when she was stepping onto a new battle-field.

At least she had an ally. Given what Abbie had heard about his heroic stint in Afghanistan, it was probably overkill in any protection stakes, but there was also the history of the bad blood between the Hunter brothers. If she and Rafael did need an intermediary, someone who was experienced in negotiating the kind of tension that represented the dark side of a loving relationship was ideal.

Not that Ethan gave much away. The slight limp he walked with, which was a legacy of his army days, attracted more than casual stares as they walked to where the ambulance was parked, but he gave no sign of being aware of the curiosity.

And when they were tucked up in the back of the ambulance, on the M4 and heading into the city, he gave no hint that Abbie might be facing any escalating complications in her life.

He and Rafael were friends but they were men. Had they shared anything more personal in the time she'd been away? A late-night card game and plenty of whisky, perhaps, along with commiseration over their disastrous love lives? Maybe Ethan had reminded Rafael that the odds had been stacked against his marriage succeeding anyway. Sure, they'd been very much in love with each other but they'd barely had time to get to know each other properly, had they? They may have chosen to get married themselves but others would no doubt have viewed it as a shot-gun wedding when they'd known that a baby was already on the way.

That baby was still asleep, bless her, now safely cocooned in the baby seat strapped onto the stretcher. Ella and Ethan sat facing her, the ambulance crew happy to sit up front, chatting, knowing that their transfer patient had a privi-leged level of medical supervision in the back.

The traffic slowed as they joined the flow on the Great West Road. A perfect opportunity to test the water, Abbie thought, but…good grief… she felt ridiculously nervous about it. She knew she couldn't just dive straight in with what was foremost on her mind but, to her dismay, her voice still came out unmistakably shaky.

'H-how are things going at the clinic?'

'Good. Very busy. You would have seen some of the publicity over our latest charity case?'

'Ah…no… Sorry, I'm a bit out of touch. I haven't seen much news for ages. Is it a paediatric case?'

'Yes. A ten-year-old Afghan girl—Anoosheh—who was noticed when her orphanage was evacuated. She got abandoned on the doorstep as a toddler when her disease became more extreme. Now she's got a neurofibromatosis that's the size of a melon and has disfigured half her face to the extent that she was being used as a servant and kept well hidden from any prospective adoptive parents that visited the orphanage. Not only that, she's probably lost the sight in one eye and is gradually losing patent airways.'

'Oh…poor thing.'

'Today's surgery won't be the last but hopefully the result will be enough to show people that there's a little girl in there who just needs to be loved. There's huge media interest and there's been some offers of adoptive homes in the UK already. I imagine there's a pack of reporters waiting to pounce on Rafael as soon as he's out of Theatre. I'll try and head them off but it's just as well he can cope with that kind of pressure while he's operating.'

'Yes…he's good at that.'

Because he could detach himself from his own emotional involvement and see the bigger picture?

The way he had even when he'd been dealing with the trauma of his own daughter's prognosis?

Abbie's heart was thumping in her chest. She took a deep breath. 'So he's…um…okay, then?'

'Seems to be.' There was a short silence, as though Ethan was debating whether to say anything more, and then he slid a brief, sideways glance at Abbie. 'I don't think I've ever seen anyone try to bury themselves in their work so effectively before. He's taken on every difficult case he could possibly squeeze into his schedule. And then some. I've barely seen him.'

Oh…no confessions of heartbreak over a card session, then. No admitting that he might have made a terrible mistake by issuing the ultimatum that if Abbie insisted on taking Ella to the States then their marriage was over.

But the argument he'd felt so passionately justified in upholding had been that their daughter's quality of life outweighed its quantity. That they didn't have the right to put her through so much extra suffering when the chances of success were so small.

Surely the fact that it *had* worked was enough to justify her decision to go? Wouldn't Rafael be so thrilled to have the prospect of Ella's long-term survival that that ultimatum was now irrelevant?

Maybe. But there was more to it, wasn't there? He was her husband and a proud man. How much damage to their relationship had she done by refusing to respect his opinion and openly defying him?

And worse than that—much worse—she'd

taken a sick baby away from her adoring father. She'd seen the pain in Rafael's eyes as she'd walked away with their daughter in her arms. He hadn't expected to see her alive again. How painful would that have been? He had every right to hate her for that.

Abbie had had Ella in her arms and she'd still cried all the way to New York.

So Rafael had shut himself away. She'd guessed that by how distant he'd sounded when she'd tried to call him. By how impersonal his email correspondence had rapidly become. He'd buried himself in his work to the extent that when Abbie had reached out in the darkest days, so far away and so lonely and so desperate for support, the response she'd received had seemed cold and clinical. As if his emotional involvement with both herself and Ella was a thing of the past.

Was it all over?

It wouldn't be fair to try and get any further clues from Ethan.

It was Rafael that Abbie needed to talk to.

Needed to *see*. The longing was getting stronger by the minute, as if her body realised that the distance between them was closing rapidly. She still loved her husband. Yes, they had pushed each other away and there was a lot to forgive on both sides, but the love was still there. It always would be.

Rafael would welcome Ella back into his life, she had no doubt at all about that. But would *she* be welcome?

The prospect of the rift between them never healing was terrifying.

With a huge effort, Abbie tried to find some inner strength. To feel positive. She even managed to find a smile to offer Ethan.

'So what else is happening? Have Leo and Lizzie set a date for the wedding yet?'

'Yes. It's going to be the last Saturday in April.'

'What? Good grief…that's only a couple of weeks away.'

'Tell me about it. A quiet affair might have

been easily organised but the kind of splash that goes with a high-society wedding at Claridge's? I'm trying to stay well out of it all.'

Abbie smiled. 'Good luck with that.'

Ethan snorted. 'Yeah… I haven't been entirely successful. Lizzie's managed to talk me into being best man. And that means I'll have to come up with some kind of speech.'

'I'm sure you can do it. Even with a tight deadline. But why are they in such a rush?'

Ethan shrugged. 'Guess they didn't want to wait. They're in love.'

There was something in Ethan's tone that made the conversation dry up completely at this point. Abbie didn't know the story behind why the Hunter brothers had been estranged for so many years but, like everyone else associated with the clinic, she was aware of the tension that still lingered between the men. The fact that Lizzie had been the one to persuade Ethan to be best man was evidence that things still weren't easy.

Was that all there was to whatever was remaining unspoken? Was Ethan happy for Leo or did he have doubts that the marriage would succeed? Maybe she and Rafael were being seen as an example of marrying in haste and repenting at leisure.

The lump in Abbie's throat made it too hard to take a new breath. To try and distract herself she leaned over Ella and stroked her baby's cheek softly with her forefinger.

The welling up of love she had for her child wasn't enough to distract her completely. She and Rafael had been in love like that once. Not very long ago, in fact. They should still be in the honeymoon phase of their marriage but look at where they were now.

What should have been a perfect union so quickly blessed with a beautiful child had been blown apart by a cruel twist of fate.

And now Abbie was returning to where it had all happened.

The pieces of that perfect life were going to be in the same place again.

What remained to be seen was whether it was going to be possible to put them back together again.

A glance through the tinted glass of the ambulance windows showed that they were passing Regent's Park. There were taxis and double-decker buses nose to tail around them. Definitely London. Home. God, it was good to be back. She could even see the big square brick building on the end of Harley Street coming up—a close neighbour of the Hunter Clinic.

Ethan followed her line of vision.

'Have you missed it?'

'So much.' But it felt distant. Like part of previous life. How hard was it going to be to find her way back?

'Are you ready to come back to work? We desperately need you as soon as you can manage and I know that they've been holding their breath to get you back on board at the Light-house.'

'I could start tomorrow.'

'Really? That would be terrific. But won't you need time to get Ella settled?'

Abbie's smile was poignant. 'The oncology ward at the Lighthouse is more of a home for Ella than anywhere else. She's spent most of her life in there. And the staff are like a huge col-lection of aunties and grannies. The sooner we get things back to normal, the better for both of us, I think.'

For all of us, she amended silently.

Rafael de Luca stripped off his bloodied gloves and dropped them in the bin. Then he pulled at his mask, breaking the strings and bending the wire that strengthened the top hem as he sent it after the gloves.

Finally, he could take a deep breath of un-filtered, fresh-feeling air. Not just because the mask was gone but because the gruelling surgery that had kept him on his feet for so many hours he'd lost count was over.

They'd done well. The team he'd gathered around him to perform this complex operation had been outstanding. In an ideal world they were maybe not exactly who he would have chosen to work so closely with but the choice of his perfect partner had been taken away when Abbie had gone, hadn't it?

The 'dream team,' they'd been known as at the Hunter Clinic. Such perfect partners in the operating theatre, it had seemed inevitable that they would find they were a perfect match outside work hours as well.

Ha...

So much for fate. And so much for a distraction from his modus operandi these days. That momentary flash of recognising what had been missing from his theatre today was as far as he would allow it to go. And that had only happened because he was so incredibly exhausted. His back ached abominably from standing in one position for far too long. His eyes ached from peering through microscopic lenses for the fine work and a generalised ache in his head from such prolonged and fierce concentration was gaining vigour.

With his gown removed and balled up to join the other disposable items in the bin, Rafael could push open the double doors and exit Theatre. With some time in hand before checking on young Anoosheh in Recovery and no concerned family to go and talk to, he could do what he most wanted and go and stand under a hot shower for a considerable period of time. He needed a shave, too.

There would be reporters anxious to hear how the surgery had gone but nobody would expect him to front up to a camera until he'd had time to clean up properly. And maybe he wouldn't have to do it at all. Rafael could see Ethan Hunter waiting outside Theatre. Far better that the media dealt with the man who was not only one of the owners of the Hunter Clinic but in charge of the charity side of the business and directly responsible for Anoosheh being brought to London for her life-changing surgery.

'Rafael… How did it go?'

'Good.' He nodded his greeting. 'As good as we could have hoped for. The tumour is gone. She has a titanium plate in her jaw and we've reconstructed her nasal passages. There's more work to be done, of course. When she's recovered from this.' The finer work of removing excess scar tissue and repositioning facial features. The kind of work Abbie excelled at.

Letting his breath out in a weary sigh, Rafael rubbed at his forehead and pinched his temples with a thumb and third finger as he screwed his eyes shut. *Dio,* but he was tired.

'And the eye?'

Rafael opened his. 'They think it may still be viable. Time will tell if she can see out of it now that the obstruction is cleared.'

'Good. That gives me enough to update the media.'

'Grazie.' Rafael found a smile. 'I appreciate you doing that. I'm going to hit the shower and then head home.' He found himself staring at Ethan's odd expression. 'What? You want me to face the cameras after all?'

'No, it's not that. It's...'

'What?' Rafael's smile was fading.

'Abbie,' Ethan said quietly.

Rafael's heart skipped a beat and then thudded painfully. Something had happened. To *Ella*? Oh, no...not that. *Si prega di dio*, not that...

'She's here, Rafael,' Ethan said into the stillness. 'They're both here. Ella's been transferred to the paediatric oncology ward here to finish her recuperation.'

Rafael could only keep staring. Why hadn't he known about this? Why hadn't Abbie contacted him? Because she couldn't even bring herself to *talk* to him any more? Was that how things were going to be now?

'It was a last-minute decision, apparently.' Ethan wasn't meeting his gaze any longer. 'The call came in after you'd started the surgery on Anoosheh. I decided it was better if you weren't distracted so I took it on myself to go and meet them at the airport. I'm sorry you didn't get the message when it was intended.'

Rafael made a noncommittal sound. This wasn't Ethan's fault. Surely the decision to transfer Ella would have been made days ago. Abbie could have let him know. Or maybe she had... He'd been so focussed on this major surgery that he hadn't checked his personal email in a day or two. He hadn't even checked in with his message service since yesterday.

And what did any of that matter anyway?

They were *here*.

Just a floor or two and a few long corridors away.

The two people who meant more to him than anyone else on this earth were in the building so what the hell was he doing, standing here?

'I have to go,' he snapped. 'I have to see them.'

The relief that a long, hot shower could provide

was forgotten. Unnecessary. A new surge of energy coursed through Rafael as he took the stairs rather than wait for a lift. Made him pick up his pace until he was almost running through the corridors in his theatre scrubs and plastic boots, earning startled glances from people who clearly thought he was on the way to an emergency.

It wasn't until he was close to the open doors leading to the paediatric oncology ward that his pace faltered. Seeing Abbie standing in the corridor outside one of the private rooms felt like he'd just run into an invisible wall.

Twelve weeks since he'd seen her.

The woman he'd married. The love of his life. The mother of his child.

But the last time he'd seen her had been when she'd walked away from him, taking their child with her. When she'd refused to bend to his ultimatum and had chosen to go against his wishes, even if it meant the end of their marriage.

When his marriage had ended.

He'd been wrong to issue that ultimatum.

Wrong to deny Ella the chance that the treatment had offered. He knew that and the knowledge was a knife that had twisted inside him for weeks now. Ever since the possibility of success had become apparent.

He also knew that Abbie had been through hell on the other side of the Atlantic and he hadn't been there to support her. He'd made her do it alone because he couldn't back down enough to find a way to apologise. Not through an email or text anyway, which had become the only way Abbie had wanted to communicate.

She must hate him for making her go through all that alone.

She hadn't seen him yet. She was looking through the window of the room. Watching to make sure Ella was asleep, perhaps, so that she could go and take enough of a break to have a meal?

She'd lost weight.

The shapely curves of her body that had first caught his eye when they'd started working together at the Lighthouse had all but disappeared. Her jeans looked too big for her legs and even from this distance he could see how prominent her collarbones were above the scooped neck of her sweater. Even the thick tresses of her glorious, honey-blond hair looked as if they'd lost volume by the way they were lying in a subdued and limp ponytail against the top of her spine.

A spine that looked a little less straight than he remembered in the strong, independent woman he'd fallen in love with and married.

How hard had this all been?

Rafael could feel his heart breaking. His every instinct was to rush forward and gather Abbie into his arms. To hold her against his heart and whisper promises. That everything would be all right. That he would always love her. That he would never allow life to be so hard for her again.

But how could he? The distance between them couldn't be resolved simply by him walking close enough to put his arms around her, and what if she pushed him away? His pride was already in tatters. Had been ever since she'd walked out on him. And, besides, there was only one of those promises that he could make with any certainty.

That he would always love her.

Would that be enough?

Maybe he was about to find out.

He never felt this nervous pushing open the doors to enter Theatre, even when he knew that the challenge was going to be huge.

His mouth never felt this dry.

It was hard to make his voice work. So hard that only a single word came out.

'Abbie...'

CHAPTER TWO

'ABBIE…'

She knew it was Rafael well before she turned
to face him. It had always been unique, the way
he said her name. It wasn't just the Italian ac-
cent or the smooth, deep voice. It was the subtle note of…wonder, almost. Or reverence? As
if she was the most wonderful woman on earth
and that made her name special, too.

Unique. One of a kind. Like Rafe.

Abbie braced herself, as she turned, for the
first sight of her husband in what suddenly
seemed a vast amount of time.

Three months.

But, at this moment, it felt like three *years*.

What would she see in his face? The joy of
knowing she'd brought his daughter back to

him? Anger that had burned away to leave a residue of resentment?

Echoes of the unbearable pain she'd seen before she'd turned her back and defiantly taken Ella away from him?

When she had turned and found herself facing Rafael with only a few feet between them, Abbie had to brace herself all over again.

How could she have forgotten the effect this man had on her? It was so much more than purely physical. More than emotional, even. It was a visceral thing. She was facing the part of her own being that had been torn free.

It stole her breath away. Made her heart stammer and trip.

'Rafe...'

Abbie tried to smile but it wasn't going to happen. Her lips simply wouldn't co-operate. She could only stare, drinking in this first glimpse, anxiously scanning his body and face to try and collect her impressions.

Dear Lord, but he looked so tired. As though

he hadn't slept well for weeks. As though he hadn't even shaved for more than a day or two. He hadn't had a haircut for a while either, and… Had he just come straight from his stint in Theatre? Black curls were flattened in places and still looked damp with sweat. Were his scrubs a size larger than he usually wore or had he lost weight?

Yes. He looked exhausted. And wary but not angry.

He looked…

Wonderful.

Tall and commanding and every bit as gorgeous as the first time she had laid eyes on him. Despite everything, Abbie could feel a curl of sensation deep in her abdomen as her body responded to being this close to him, but this overwhelming awareness wasn't anything as simple as physical attraction.

They knew each other so well. On so many levels. They made up two halves of a whole.

They *loved* each other.

At least, they had.

If only Rafael would smile. Or step closer. Hold his arms open so that she could fall into an embrace that would magically erase the pain they'd caused each other and make everything all right again.

But he wasn't moving. He seemed to be staring back at her with a mirror image of her intense scrutiny of him.

'How are you, Abbie?'

'I'm...' The word 'fine' tried to form on her lips but it wasn't true. Abbie didn't feel fine at all. She felt overwhelmed and unsure. 'I'm... okay. A bit tired. It's been a big day.'

A big twelve weeks.

A traumatic journey that she'd had to take *alone*. Abbie swallowed hard as she felt the hurt coalesce into the shape of the painful rock inside her chest that she'd lived with for so long now. 'And you? How are you, Rafe?'

'I'm...also okay...I think.' The familiar gesture as Rafael raked his hair with his fingers made the rock shift a little and sent a painful shaft through Abbie's heart. He was as over-whelmed as she was with this reunion. Unsure of what to say. Or do. 'I…wasn't expecting this. It's…'

'Sudden, I know.' This was weird. To feel the hurt this man had caused her and yet to feel so much compassion for him at the same time. 'I would have let you know sooner but it…just hap-pened.'

He didn't believe her and Abbie could under-stand that. The possibility of sending Ella back to her home town to continue her recuperation had only been talked about in the last few days. She was still fragile. How much organisation had been needed to send a sick baby to another country?

'They only started to make enquiries first thing this morning. And things just fell into place. There was space available on a flight and a bed here at the Lighthouse and they didn't have to arrange a medical escort. And…when her results came through later, looking so good, Dr Goldstein just looked at me and smiled and he said…he said, "How 'bout it, Mom? Would you like to go home today?" And…'

And Abbie's voice was shaking now. Could she tell him that the first thing she'd thought at that point had been how badly she'd wanted to see *him* again? That the picture in her head of Rafael holding his baby daughter again and seeing how much better she looked had filled her heart with so much longing that it had felt like it might burst?

No. She couldn't tell him because he had started speaking himself. She had to stop saying anything. Rafael had to repeat his question.

'What results? What were the tests?'

Did it matter? This was a doctor talking, not a father. Was he still that distant? This was what had caused their separation in the first place, wasn't it? The way he could remove himself from the emotional involvement of being a parent. To step back and see the bigger picture through a professional lens. To decide that the quality of what would be a very short life was more important than the desperation to keep your own child alive as long as humanly possible.

'They took a bone-marrow biopsy yesterday. And bloods. We already knew she'd got through the dangerous cytokine release syndrome that the treatment caused. What we didn't know was whether the T cell therapy was really working.'

'And…' It looked as though Rafael was having to swallow a large lump in his throat, judging by the way the muscles in his jaw and neck were working. 'It's looking good?'

That was more like it. The doctor would want the exact figures. A copy of the test results, like the one Abbie had ready for him in her bag. But for a father? Knowing that the results were *good* would be enough to create such a wash of relief and hope for the future that the numbers were irrelevant.

Abbie nodded. It took a moment to trust her voice. 'She still needs protection for her immune system and she'll need another bone-marrow biopsy at the three-month mark but…' She took a deep breath as she blinked back tears. 'It's looking good, Rafe. As good as I hoped it would. The treatment's worked.'

As good as *she'd* hoped?

The choice of pronoun pushed him away. Just as Rafael had been about to pull Abbie into his arms so that they could celebrate this miraculous milestone together as Ella's parents.

To rush into the room they were standing outside and see for himself that Ella wasn't the critically ill baby she'd been the last time he'd seen her.

But it was true. He deserved to be dismissed as having been one of the hopeful parents. As soon as Abbie had heard about the experimental treatment that took T cells from the blood and reengineered them in a laboratory so that they could be put back into the body to find and kill the cancerous leukaemia cells, the hope had been born on her side.

All Rafael had been able to see had been how experimental the treatment was. That the success rates with adults had not been consistent and it had *never* been tried in a baby. That the risks were enormous and going through with the treatment would only cause so much more suffering that would probably still end in Ella's death. And he'd been right. The new T cells had caused an illness that had come within a heartbeat of killing Ella. She'd hovered between life and death in a paediatric intensive-care unit for weeks.

And *he* should have been there but he hadn't been able to bring himself to travel so far in order to watch his baby die. And, yes...even though it shamed him to admit it, part of what had kept him here had been that it seemed like a fitting punishment for Abbie for taking his beloved child away from him.

So much pain. On both sides.

What would Abbie do if he tried to take her in his arms right now? Push him away? Flinch?

He couldn't bear it if that happened.

But somehow he had to try and find a way to bridge this awful gap between them.

'It's been so long, Abbie. So...*hard*...'

So hard. It had been a nightmare ever since their precious baby had hit the headlines at becoming one of the rare cases of ALL being diagnosed at such an early age. Gruelling months of chemotherapy that had failed to produce remission, let alone a cure. And having them both disappear from his life had only plunged him deeper into his personal hell, especially in the wake of the fights over whether it was the right thing to do.

Missing his wife every day but being so angry at the way she'd made things so much worse. Missing his child with an ache that had gone even deeper than his bones. Sleepless nights and days waiting for the phone call that would deliver the dreaded news that the battle had been lost. Days when a fierce focus on his work had been the only thing that had kept him sane.

He heard the way Abbie's breath left her lungs in an incredulous huff. The pain he could see in her eyes hit him like a physical blow.

'How would you know, Rafe? You weren't *there*.'

Would they ever be able to get past this?

'I'm here now.' His voice sounded as raw as it felt. 'Isn't that enough?'

Abbie just stared at him for the longest time. He could see her lips tremble as her hands gripped the opposite arms, crossed over her breasts as if she was defending her heart.

'No,' she whispered. 'I don't think it is.' She took a ragged, inward breath. 'We…needed you, Rafe. And you…you weren't there.'

Dio, but this was hard. Did they have to go through it all again? Every impassioned fight? He'd never felt this tired in his life.

'You know why.'

'Yes.' Abbie's voice was tight. 'I know *why*.

But I still don't *understand*. How could you not be there if you really love someone?' There were tears on her face now but Rafael couldn't move to brush them away. He'd lost the right to offer comfort because he'd caused the pain.

'You weren't there,' Abbie said again. 'For me *or* Ella. And…and it was *awful*, Rafe… You have no idea.…'

'That's not true.' He couldn't help the hard edge that made the words clipped. But it seemed like they did have to go over the old ground just to get to a place where they could talk to each other again. 'I have a very good idea. That's why I didn't want you to go. To put Ella through that.'

Flashes of pain from other, long-ago cases were never far away. Especially cases like little Freddie.… Years ago, now, but it was still an effort to push the memory of that particular little boy away. Rafael had started in paediatric oncology determined to beat death for those innocent children but he'd learned the hard way that there had to be limits. That fighting *too* hard could only make things worse for everyone involved. Including the surgeon. He'd had to leave the specialty in the end because the toll it had taken on him personally had been too great.

'And if I hadn't, we wouldn't be here now. Ella wouldn't still be alive.'

'No…' The word was a weary sigh.

This was also true. And suddenly nothing else mattered. Ella was still alive. She was in the room right beside him. He couldn't stay out here a moment longer. Taking a step closer to the door brought him a step closer to Abbie, but she moved a little. And now Rafael could see through the window of the room.

He could see *Ella*.

Sitting in a cot and playing happily with a toy.

A toy he recognised. Called Ears. A soft pink rabbit with disproportionately long legs and ears. A silly toy he'd bought when she'd first been sick and been admitted here, which had fast become her 'cuddly.'

Ella was holding Ears in one hand as she knelt

in the cot and then pulled herself up using the side of the cot. He could see the nasal prongs supplying oxygen taped to her face and one arm was bandaged, keeping the IV line that went to the port beneath her collarbone safe from being tugged. It didn't stop her getting to her feet, though.

Dio…she was strong enough to stand?

It didn't stop Ears being dropped over the side of the cot either, but Ella didn't burst into instant tears, like most children her age would. She just looked down at the floor and then up, perfectly confident that help would not be far away.

And then Rafael could really see her face for the first time. Those big, dark eyes were looking straight at him.

For a long, long moment they stared at each other. Rafael could remember the first time he'd held this baby and the overwhelming need to protect her. He could remember the feel of her downy skin. The smell of her when she'd been freshly bathed and fed. The sound of her voice when she'd been learning her own baby language.

But would she remember anything at all about him?

It seemed that she did. Her eyes got even bigger and those rosebud lips curled and curved into a smile. And Ella held up her little arms, which was enough to make her lose her balance and sit down on her padded bottom with a thump, but she was still smiling.

Still holding out her arms to her father.

And nothing else mattered.

Without even another glance at Abbie, Rafael rushed into the room.

Abbie stood and watched through the window.

It had been only a few minutes since she'd been doing exactly this, watching to see if Ella would be happy for a few minutes while she went to… What had she been going to do? Go to the bathroom? Make a coffee in the staffroom?

Whatever her intention had been, she'd forgotten it the moment she'd heard Rafael call her name and she'd had to brace herself for their reunion.

And now it was over.

They'd seen each other again. They'd talked.

But had anything been resolved?

If anything, Abbie felt more unsure than before.

Slow tears were leaking from her eyes and rolling down the side of her nose as she watched Rafael gather up his daughter into his arms and press his cheek against the top of her head. He had his eyes closed so he couldn't see that she was watching. And…oh, God…did he have tears tracing the edge of *his* nose, too? No…Rafael would never cry. But if he ever did, his face would look exactly the way it did right now.

The love he had for his daughter was almost as palpable as the wall Abbie had to reach out and touch for support.

He'd never expected to be able to hold her again, had he?

Or to see her smile. To hear that noise she made when she was really happy—a kind of cross between cooing and giggling that sounded like water going out of a sink.

Being a plughole, they'd called it. *Ella's being a plughole*, they'd tell each other and then they'd both hold each other's gaze and smile because they knew it was such a happy noise and it had been such a rare thing amongst the pain and sickness. Those poignant smiles and the silent communication of eye contact had been moments of connection that had given them strength to go on. That had made them feel that sharing this heartbreaking journey was making their relationship stronger. But, in the end, like it did so often with this kind of unimaginable stress, it had torn them apart.

Yes. Rafael still adored his daughter. She could see him rocking her now and hear his voice as he spoke rapidly in Italian. She caught the word *fiorella*. Ella's proper name. His little flower. And he was singing now. Softly. Still in Italian.

Stroking the odd patches of wispy hair on Ella's head so gently. It was one of the things she loved about this man, that he could be so passionate. So demonstrative.

And for a moment when he'd been out here with her, he'd looked as if he still loved *her* like that, too.

Just before he'd stupidly said how *hard* it had been for him.

He hadn't been there. Hadn't sat for countless hours amongst the bank of monitors in the intensive-care unit, wondering if each breath Ella took would be her last.

Maybe she shouldn't have taken the bait and reignited the old conflict but…it still *hurt*, dammit.

It wasn't going to just go away by itself.

Being together in the same place wasn't enough because it felt like there was no common ground between them.

Or if there was, the only person inhabiting it was a baby called Ella.

CHAPTER THREE

'I CAN'T BELIEVE you're starting back at work so soon.' Ella's nurse for today, Melanie, was watching Abbie spoon morsels of breakfast into her daughter's mouth. 'You've only just set foot back in the country.'

'I just want to get back to normal.' Abbie's smile was a bit of an effort. Getting Ella back to London had been a huge step closer to getting back to a normal life but she had no real idea what 'normal' was going to be from now on.

She caught an escaping dollop of porridge with the edge of the plastic spoon and waited until Ella opened her mouth so she could pop it back where it belonged. 'And I've had far too much time away already,' she added. 'You know what they say, Mel. "Use it or lose it."'

Melanie looked up from the drugs she was preparing for Ella's syringe driver. 'You won't go straight back into full time, though, will you?'

Abbie's headshake was swift. There was no way she could suddenly cope with that kind of punishing schedule—the long surgery hours at the Lighthouse, outpatient clinics, ward rounds and the travel time and consultations at the Hunter Clinic. A schedule that Rafael had apparently ramped up to an unthinkable level while she'd been away. No work–life balance there but she could understand escaping like that. And her own life had been just as one-sided. For a very long time.

'I haven't been genuinely full-time for ages,' she said aloud. 'We started scaling things down when I got to about six months pregnant and then things got even more disrupted after Ella was born, of course.'

Melanie's nod was sympathetic. She clicked the syringe into the driver. 'You must be missing your work, too. You don't get to be as good as you are if you don't really love what you're doing. Are you in Theatre today?'

'No. It's just an outpatient clinic this morning. They're easing me in gently.'

'That's good.' Melanie was making an exaggerated happy face at Ella. 'You done yet, chicken? Ready to have a wash and get dressed and face the day?'

Abbie wiped Ella's face with a damp cloth. 'I think we both are.' With a final cuddle she handed Ella to Melanie. 'Be good, sweetheart. I'll be back as soon as I can.'

Setting off to the Lighthouse's outpatient department, she realised how nervous she was feeling. Maybe it was because she was out of her jeans for the first time in ages and wearing clothes more appropriate for her job. A neat blouse tucked into a long, swirly skirt that reached the top of her boots. An unbuttoned white coat as a jacket. The bright name badge that had a cute flower with a smiley face for a centre that told the world she was 'Doctor Abbie.'

Or maybe it was because people would be bringing their precious children to her to have decisions made about potentially major surgery. She would have to weigh up the risks versus benefits for other people's children when she was so acutely aware of how it felt to be a parent herself. What the repercussions of those risks might be.

Oh, for heaven's sake, Abbie scolded herself. 'It's only an outpatient clinic. Hardly life or death.'

There was an expectation, however, that she would start again with the really high-pressure work as soon as possible and get up to reasonable speed so that she wouldn't lose the skills that had won her such a prestigious position in the first place. The expectation wasn't just coming from the Hunter brothers or the head of the paediatric surgical department at the Lighthouse Children's Hospital.

It was coming from Abbie herself and that was

why she'd told Ethan that she would start again so soon.

The passion that had led her into this career represented a part of herself that she had no intention of losing. First and foremost, it was who she was. Being a wife and a mother might be just as important but that part of her couldn't survive in isolation. Not happily, anyway, and if she wasn't happy she couldn't do her best. *Be* her best.

This nervousness that made her stomach churn was very unfamiliar, though. Disconcerting. It was only an outpatient clinic she was heading for, she reminded herself again. One of her favourite parts of her job, where she could spend time with young patients and their families, either exploring the possible routes they could take to make a positive difference in their lives or checking up on progress and getting the satisfaction of seeing that difference.

Why was she so nervous?

Because she felt rusty from being away from

the action for too long? Those kinds of nerves might be expected when she was back in Theatre with a scalpel in her hand but they would be welcome then because she'd know they would keep her focussed and would evaporate as her confidence returned.

This was different. This was the first time she would be working with Rafael since she'd accepted the ultimatum that meant their marriage was over. Would working together make things better or worse? Could it break through the polite distance they'd ended up in last night before Rafael had excused himself to do a post-operative check on his most recent patient?

Apparently not.

Rafael had arrived before Abbie and, against the background of a crowded waiting room, he was sorting files with the clinic's nurse manager, Nicky. Like Abbie, he was wearing an unbuttoned white coat over his professional uniform of tidy trousers and a neat shirt and tie. He had a name badge on his pocket, too. Nothing as frivolous as a smiling flower, though. His was a far more dignified standard issue with the tiny lighthouse logo and his full name.

Abbie hadn't even offered to get him a fun badge when she'd had her own made. She'd always known the limits to which his pride would let him bend.

Or she'd thought she'd known. Until it had come to the crunch.

Both Rafael and the nurse manager looked up as Abbie approached.

'Abbie.' Nicky's smile was welcoming. 'It's so good to see you. I was delighted to hear that you'd be sharing the clinic this morning. I'll bet your registrar was delighted as well.'

Rafael's smile wasn't nearly as welcoming as Nicky's but at least it *was* a smile. One that was at odds with the wary look in his eyes. Surely Rafael wasn't nervous about working with *her* again? No...

She'd never known him to be nervous about anything. Excited, certainly, like he'd been when they'd seen the stripes on the pregnancy test stick that had meant they were on the way to becoming parents. Fearful, maybe, like he'd been when they'd been waiting for those first test results to come back and explain why their newborn baby was failing to thrive in such a dramatic fashion. And angry, definitely, like he'd been when she'd refused to accept his decision that enough was enough when it came to putting Ella through any more misery.

But nervous? This was disconcerting. Abbie had to force herself to return Nicky's smile of welcome.

'I did hear that you've been incredibly busy. It's lovely to see you, too, Nicky.'

'And I hear that Ella's doing well. That's such good news.'

'It certainly is.' Abbie slid a sideways glance at Rafael but he seemed absorbed in the list of patients. He eased a set of patient notes out of a pile and put it to one side.

'How long before you can take her home?'

Rafael's head jerked up at this query and Abbie could feel the intensity of his glance and it felt... accusing? This wasn't something they'd had a chance to talk about last night. How could they, when Abbie wasn't even sure whether she *had* a home to take Ella back to?

'Um...it'll be a few weeks, I think. We need to see how things go. Certainly no decision will be made until she's had her T cells checked at the three-month mark.'

Which gave them some breathing space at least. Time to sort out where they were as far as their marriage went. Or how they might share Ella's parenting in the future.

The noise level in the waiting room was increasing. A scuffle had broken out near the toy box and more than one child was crying. A woman carrying a well-wrapped baby was standing near the door and looking as if she would prefer to turn around and go out again. Her partner was trying to persuade her to take a seat. Nicky surveyed the scene and squared her shoulders.

'We'd better get this show on the road. I'll get the first patients into the consulting rooms. I've put you in Room 3, Abbie.'

'Cheers.'

As Nicky moved away, it felt as if Abbie and Rafael were almost alone, sandwiched between the waiting-room chaos and the rest of the staff, who were busy organising the rooms for the consultations and tests that were scheduled.

'Hi...' Abbie offered a smile. 'You okay?'

'I'm fine.' Rafael smiled back. Another polite smile. 'And you? That chair in Ella's room can't be that comfortable to sleep in.'

'I'm used to it. I've been sleeping in one of those chairs for so long now that a bed will probably feel weird.'

And there it was again. A slap in the face. A reminder of where she'd been for the last three months. An echo of the awkward moment last night when Rafael had asked if she would come home to sleep and she'd said that changing something that big in Ella's routine was out of the question just yet.

'How is she this morning?'

'Good. She ate a little stewed apple and porridge for breakfast. It's great that she already knows so many of the nurses on the ward. She's got Melanie today and I don't think she even noticed me leaving to come here.'

'I'll get up and see her as soon as we've finished here. I...wasn't sure whether to disturb your early-morning routine.'

Keeping his distance? Abbie stifled a sigh. 'She's your daughter, Rafe. You can spend as much time with her as you want.'

His nod was almost curt. He reached for a pile of notes and slid them along the counter. 'Here are your patients for this morning.'

It wasn't rocket science to see that her pile was much smaller than his. Or that the names on the list had been divided far more equally. Abbie raised her eyebrows. Rafael shrugged.

'I've added some cases to my list. It's your first morning back, Abbie. I wanted to make things a little easier for you.'

Abbie stared at him. 'If I didn't think I could cope, I wouldn't be here.'

The words came out a little more vehemently than she'd intended but it was bad enough feeling nervous about her own performance. She didn't need other people doubting her abilities.

He mirrored her raised eyebrows and gave another one of those subtle shrugs that was part of what kept people so aware of his birthplace. *As you wish*, it said. *It's of no importance to me.*

Except it had been of importance or he wouldn't have done it. And it was a generous gesture when he probably had too much to do today anyway. Maybe she should compromise. Abbie scanned the list rapidly.

'I'd like to keep this little girl.' She tapped the list. 'Grade-three microtia. That's one of my favourite things to do.'

Rafael knew that. He'd been in Theatre with

her more than once as she'd tackled the delicate surgery to create an ear from the birth deformity that had left nothing more than a peanut-shaped blob as an outer ear. Life-changing surgery for a child who was being teased at school, and this little girl was seven years old.

'And this one…' She pulled another set of notes from the pile. 'Seven-month-old ready for repair of his cleft lip and palate. Oh…it's Angus. I remember us seeing him for his first consultation. That's another one I'd love to do…'

Her voice trailed away. The sometimes massive surgery needed to correct this kind of birth defect was a procedure that both she and Rafael were known to be exceptionally good at. Together. Rafael's skill at shifting bones and moulding features in conjunction with her ability to join tiny blood vessels and nerves and then suture to leave almost invisible scars had made them a team that people came from all over the country to consult via the Hunter Clinic.

Would she want to do it by herself?

'Maybe I'll leave this one for you.' Abbie couldn't bring herself to look up at Rafael. 'I'll take Harriet back, though. I've been wondering how those burn scars are settling. She must be due for her next surgery.'

Rafael simply nodded, took the first set of notes from his pile and headed to the first consulting room. Abbie took her first set and went past his door to Room 3. Separate lists. Separate rooms. Separate operating theatres even? Was this how it was going to be from now on?

Even when they'd seen different patients in the past, they'd always been popping into each other's rooms to get a second opinion or simply brainstorm a case. This felt wrong but it was also a relief. Perhaps they needed time to get used to working together again. Or maybe they actually needed to find out if they *could* work together when their personal lives were in such disarray. Being too close too soon could well mean that it would never happen.

There was no reason why they couldn't define

some professional boundaries and make it work. Was there?

Apparently there was. The message Abbie got later that day, asking her to attend a meeting at the Hunter Clinic, had all the undertones of a 'Please explain.'

'Urgent message, Mr de Luca.'

'What is it, Nicole?' The expression on the young woman's face suggested that his secretary was anxious. She was right behind him as he kept moving into his office.

'A meeting at the Hunter Clinic at five p.m. With Leo and Ethan Hunter. In Leo's office. Gwen said she's checked your calendar and you're available, so...'

The sentence was left hanging but Nicole might as well have finished it. The unsaid words were that no excuses would be acceptable short of the direst emergency.

'Did she say what it was about?'

'No. Shall I order a cab for you?'

'I suppose you'll have to,' Rafael growled. He didn't have any consultations booked at the exclusive Hunter Clinic that he could think of so he had no idea why it was suddenly so important to meet with the Hunter brothers this afternoon, and if he did have a space on his calendar, he'd much rather be spending that time with Ella.

Now he'd barely have time to eat the sandwich he'd just bought on the run for a late lunch. He dropped the plastic triangular package on his desk, along with the other purchase he'd made in the gift shop beside the café.

'Oh, what's that?' Nicole's face lit up with a wide smile. 'It's gorgeous.' She reached out to pick up the huge teddy bear that was wearing a sparkly pink tutu and had pink ballet shoes on its feet. She hugged the bear. 'I love it. It's so soft and squishy. And *huge*. It must be just as big as Ella is now.'

'Almost.' It wasn't really a baby's toy either, but his Fiorella was growing up, wasn't she?

'I heard she was back. And that she's doing well. That's wonderful, isn't it?'

'It certainly is.'

Nicole put the bear down with some reluctance. 'She'll want to be a dancer when she grows up after she sees this. Look at those cute ballet shoes. Oh…I would have loved something like this when I was a little girl.'

A little girl. Not a baby any more. Yes… He had been shocked by how much Ella had changed since he'd last seen her. It was mainly due to such an improvement in her condition but three months was a long time in a baby's life. She had more teeth and her smile looked different. Her hands were so much cleverer and her baby babble was beginning to have the inflections of real speech. She could stand up and even walk if someone held her hands. She'd barely been able to sit unaided when he'd last seen her.

He'd missed so much and that added another painful layer to the guilt he already felt at having left Abbie to cope alone in New York.

Rafael tried to shake his swift train of thought. 'Order the taxi for four-thirty,' he instructed Nicole, picking up the bear and depositing it in a corner of the office. 'I don't want to get stuck in rush-hour traffic. Anything else urgent I should know about?'

'No.'

'Good. I'll get on with my clinic notes, then.'

Except that the pink bear sitting in the corner kept catching his peripheral vision. Making him think of Ella.

And of Abbie.

Would she forgive him for leaving her to cope alone in New York like that? For sending her away with the threat that their marriage was finished? It wasn't the time to push too hard right now. Not when she was exhausted and trying to get settled back into being in London. When she not only had Ella to care for but she was starting work again as well. He wanted to help but between Abbie and the wonderful staff on the paediatric oncology ward there was nothing he could do there. It hadn't gone down very well when he'd tried to lighten Abbie's workload at the outpatient clinic this morning either.

And she didn't seem to be making any effort to close the distance between them. She hadn't even followed him into the room when he'd rushed in to see Ella yesterday, and ever since then it had felt like she was enclosed in a bubble. There but not there.

It was frustrating.

So was fighting London traffic to get to the Hunter Clinic by 5:00 p.m. It wouldn't have been so bad if he could have gone home after this meeting because home was in Primrose Hill, about halfway between the Lighthouse and Harley Street, where the Hunter Clinic was located. But he had to get back to the Lighthouse as soon as he could because he still had patients to see, including Anoosheh. Apparently she was running a slight temperature and there was concern about potential infection. His entire day had run a little behind schedule thanks to taking on extra outpatients to ease the load on Abbie this morning.

Rafael desperately wanted to spend time with Ella, too. As long as possible. He wanted to give her the bear and see if it made her smile. If it didn't, he would have to go looking for something else. What *did* make her smile these days? What did she like best of all to eat? What songs did she like to have sung to her?

There was so much he needed to find out.

And home wasn't really home any more, anyway, was it? It hadn't been, from the moment Abbie had walked away from that final, dreadful row, when he'd told her that if she took Ella to New York, their marriage was over.

Oh, her clothes still hung in the wardrobe and her books were still in the bookshelves. It was still the same gorgeous period-conversion apartment that they'd both fallen in love with and purchased in the week before their wedding. It still had the same fabulous view towards the Regent's Canal and the bonus of the private courtyard garden that boasted a tree.

A tree they'd put a baby's swing in to celebrate the six-month mark of Abbie's pregnancy. A swing that had never been used. It had collected leaves in autumn and been filled with snow in the winter. Now it just hung there, too bright for a garden that had yet to blossom for spring. A cruel reminder of what could have been.

All these things taunted Rafael now so he spent as little time as possible in the apartment. He couldn't stay there if their marriage was truly over. Maybe Abbie would want to live there with Ella. So that she could use the swing...

'This is fine.' Rafael rapped on the glass partition to alert the cab driver. 'I can walk from here.'

Giving the driver a generous tip, Rafael took his briefcase and umbrella and strode down Harley Street, his long coat flapping. He should button it up to protect his suit because the leaden sky looked as if it could open at any moment but he was in too much of a hurry. The usual reverence the old buildings in this street instilled was gone, too. He didn't even glance at any of the brass plaques that advertised the famous medical people who had once worked in these fabulous old buildings.

The facade of the Hunter Clinic, at 200 Harley Street, blended seamlessly with its historic neighbours but the interior made it look more like an exclusive hotel than a clinic. The heels of his Italian shoes tapped on a polished marble floor as Rafael marched through the huge reception area, past the inviting white sofas bathed in soft light from the table lamps beside them.

Only Helen, the senior receptionist, was on duty at the moment. In her late forties, Helen was always immaculately groomed and conveyed just the sort of welcome the clinic wanted. Capable, calm and compassionate. Weren't those words in the clinic's mission statement some-where?

'Mr de Luca.' Helen's smile held no disap-proval of the fact that he was nearly ten min-utes late. 'How lovely that you could make it. They're all ready for you in Leo's office.'

Leo's office? They were *all* ready for him?

What the hell was going on here?

Leo was the older of the two brothers—sons of the celebrated plastic surgeon, James Hunter. Rafael had never delved too deeply into the scan-dal that had surrounded James's death. He only knew that it was through the tireless efforts of Leo that the clinic had survived and the cloud had been lifted from the Hunter name. He also knew that a huge rift had appeared between the brothers when Ethan had joined the army and left Leo to fight alone to save the clinic, but that was in the past, wasn't it?

Ethan was back. And Leo had finally settled for one woman.

These were happier times for the Hunter

brothers. So why weren't they looking happy right now?

And what, *in nome di dio*, was *Abbie* doing here?

She looked pale. Frightened, almost. Rafael hadn't seen her look like this since that terrible time when they had been waiting for the first results to find out what was wrong with their tiny baby. What had Leo and Ethan said or done to make her look like this now?

How *dared* they?

The need to protect Abbie was sudden and fierce. Rafael dropped his briefcase and umbrella on the nearest chair but he didn't sit down. He didn't take his coat off. Instead, he stepped behind Abbie's chair and gripped the back of the seat.

'What's going on?' he snapped.

Had they fired her? Because she couldn't give the kind of focussed dedication to her job that she'd been known for before she'd become a mother?

Before she'd become his wife?

Surely not. Everyone here at the clinic, especially these brothers, had done all they could to support the de Luca family through the crisis. They'd given Abbie unlimited paid leave. Helped enormously with the logistical details and appalling expenses that Ella's treatment in the States had engendered.

He shouldn't have let them be so involved. This was *his* family.

He would look after them.

No matter if Abbie had been fired. He could support them. *All* of them. He would protect them. With his life, if necessary.

The Hunter brothers exchanged a glance. It was Leo who spoke.

'Sit down, Rafael. Take your coat off for a minute. This won't take long.'

'I do not *want* to sit down.' The anger was building rapidly. 'I want to know what you've said to my *wife* to make her look so upset.'

He heard Abbie's sharp intake of breath at his

tone. Or was it the way he'd referred to her as his 'wife'—as if she were some kind of possession?

Rafael closed his eyes and took a deep, inward breath as he deliberately dialled down his anger. Whatever was going on, becoming too passionate about it would only make things worse. Hadn't he learned that lesson already?

Towering over everybody else in this room wasn't going to help anything either.

Opening his eyes again, Rafael inclined his head in acquiescence that something clearly needed to be dealt with and he moved to lower his body into the empty seat beside Abbie.

He took a sideways glance at her, still concerned by how pale she looked, but Abbie was staring down at her hands. He wanted her to look at *him* so that he could send her a silent message that everything would be all right. *He* would deal with whatever it was that had prompted their summons into this office.

There was a beat of silence in the room and then Ethan cleared his throat.

'We asked you both to come in this afternoon,' he said into the silence, 'because an issue has been brought to our attention that we thought needed urgent resolution. A complaint has been made—'

'Che cosa?' Rafael's gaze jerked to meet Ethan's. 'What are you talking about?'

'It's not a complaint, exactly.' Leo flicked an unreadable glance at his brother. 'I would phrase it more as an expression of disappointment that a client feels strongly enough about to bring it to our attention.'

'I have no idea what you're talking about,' Rafael snapped. 'Is someone unhappy with my work? And why is Abbie here?' The speed of his speech was increasing. So was the volume. 'Nobody could have complained about her work because she hasn't even been in the country for three months.' Rafael shook his head in frustration and tried to calm down again. 'Or is that what this "disappointment" is about? The fact that we have had to deal with a family crisis that has disrupted our ability to work?'

Again the brothers exchanged a meaningful glance.

'You could say that,' Leo said. 'Sort of.'

'Spit it out, man,' Rafael growled. 'I'm hoping to have enough time after my *work* to visit my daughter before she's asleep for the night.'

'Of course.' Leo turned to smile at Abbie. 'And can I just say again how wonderful it is to have you and Ella back? Especially when you've come back with such a great result.'

'Thanks, Leo.' Abbie's nod was stiff. She caught Rafael's gaze briefly then and he could see that she was just as mystified as he was by the reason for this meeting.

Ethan took his cue from Leo's nod. He looked directly at Rafael, who had the strange impression that a game of 'good cop, bad cop' was going on here. And Ethan had been designated 'bad cop.'

'I believe you saw the MacDonald family at

your outpatient clinic this morning? With their seven-month-old son, Angus, who's now ready for admission for repair of his bilateral cleft lip and palate?'

'That is correct.' Rafael frowned. What on earth had the MacDonalds found to complain about? 'They seemed perfectly happy to know how well the stretching and reshaping of the tissues has been with the taping and use of the retainer. He's a good candidate for a single initial surgery to repair the defects in both his lip and palate.'

'He'll still need further surgery for cosmetic improvements, though.' It was Abbie who spoke.

It was Abbie who'd first seen Angus back when the newborn had been brought down from Scotland by his distressed parents. She'd immediately called Rafael to share the consultation and reassure them that they would be able to achieve an almost perfect result for their son.

He nodded. 'You can deal with that further

down the track. And I'll do the gum repair later. When Angus is around seven years old.'

Ethan had listened to the exchange and was shaking his head. Rafael glared at him. 'The MacDonalds were delighted to know that their son can be admitted for the surgery as early as the end of the week. What *is* the problem here?'

'The MacDonalds came to the Hunter Clinic for a private consultation within weeks of Angus being born,' Ethan said. 'Do you know why they chose us out of all the places they could have taken their baby for surgery after they'd decided they didn't want to go on a National Health waiting list?'

'We treat a lot of these types of cases,' Rafael responded. 'Our reputation is very good.'

'No.' It was Leo who was shaking his head this time. 'Our reputation for dealing with this particular birth defect is the *best*. And you know why?'

Rafael met his gaze squarely. 'My background in craniofacial surgery for paediatric oncology patients gave me a very good training that has easily transferred to birth defects.' He shrugged, still puzzled. 'I'm good at what I do.'

Repair of this kind of deformity that was so distressing to parents wasn't just about the re-shaping of bones and tissues, though, was it? How good the final result was was largely dependent on the skill of the plastic surgeon involved in the finer, external work.

'And Abbie's very good at what *she* does,' he added. 'The best, in fact.'

'Exactly.' Leo and Ethan exchanged a satisfied glance this time. 'And therein lies our issue.'

Rafael raised an eyebrow.

'You saw the MacDonalds this morning.'

'Yes. You know this already.'

'But Abbie didn't see them. We understand that the case had been on her list, with a note to share the consultation with you. But you...ah... rearranged the lists this morning.'

'Only so that Abbie wasn't overwhelmed with work on her first day back.'

'You also told the MacDonalds that you would be performing the whole surgery. Alone. That Abbie would not be available to work with you on the case.'

'Ah…' Rafael could feel Abbie's stare. She wasn't happy. But it had been her choice to let him shift the case onto his list this morning. Women! *Dio*… The way their minds worked was an unfathomable mystery sometimes.

'The MacDonalds came to the Hunter Clinic because of the reputation that both of you have in dealing with a case like theirs. The emphasis here is on *both* of you. They'd heard about the Hunter Clinic's "dream team." Now they're feeling…cheated.'

'Look…' Leo sounded uncomfortable. 'We're well aware of your personal issues but whatever problems you have need to be put aside in working hours for the benefit of the clinic, not to mention the benefit of our clients.'

'There's a waiting list of elective cases like this,' Ethan added swiftly. 'And an even longer list of potential charity cases. This is an incredibly common birth defect.'

'We can't support this separation at a professional level,' Leo put in. 'You have to be able to work together.'

'We were working together,' Abbie said. 'This morning. And, yes, Rafe did take the MacDonald case off my list but I had the choice. I *could* have kept it.'

'You're missing the point,' said Ethan. 'It's not a case of who gets who. Even a few minutes ago you were both talking about future surgery that Angus would need like it was some kind of "pass the parcel" game. That might be all very well with elective cases but what's going to happen with an acute case? An emergency? Are you two going to be squabbling in a corner because you're not professional enough to work on the same case? In the same theatre? *Together*?'

'No.' Abbie's voice sounded strangled.

'Of course not.' Rafael was insulted. 'That suggestion is *ridicolo...*'

'You were a tight team,' Leo said quietly. 'The best. We want that back.'

'Everybody knows how tough it's been,' Ethan said. 'And we've all done our best to help but the worst is over now and the kind of disruption we've seen today can't be allowed to happen again.' He shook his head. 'If word gets out that you two are not happy working together, it will cause untold damage to our reputation and we're not going to allow that to happen.'

Leo sighed. 'If it continues, we might all have to rethink whether you can continue in your current employment.' He eyed Abbie. 'You've been a full-time mother for months now. If that's more important to you than your career then we'll find a way to work around it, but you need to be up front with us.'

'I am being up front with you.' Abbie's voice was shaky. 'And I've never considered choosing to give up my work. My daughter is the most important person in the world to me but I know how brilliant the childcare system at the Lighthouse is. We'd always planned to juggle our careers and family life to allow us to both continue working.'

Rafael felt something tighten inside his chest. He remembered those planning sessions. Lying on the bed beside Abbie, admiring the increasing size of her belly. Keeping his hand resting lightly on her skin so that he could marvel at the movement he could feel beneath it. Imagining them both collecting their baby from the crèche and taking her home for family time.

Life had been so perfect back then. So full of exciting dreams for the future.

How had it all turned to dust? He wanted it back. All of it.

But Abbie wasn't even looking in his direction again now. She was facing her employers here at the clinic. Fighting for her *career*.

'Then the issue is simply whether you can continue working together.' Both Ethan and Leo shifted their gaze from Abbie to Rafael. Abbie also turned to look at him.

'I can,' she said.

There was determination in her eyes. And something more.

Hope that this could be a way through the enormous barrier that still lay between them?

Or was that wishful thinking on his part?

Whatever. It was a first step.

Rafael smiled. 'So can I,' he said. 'I look forward to the privilege of working with you again, Abbie.'

CHAPTER FOUR

SHE HADN'T EXPECTED THIS.

She'd been in perfect agreement with Leo and Ethan during that meeting this afternoon. Okay, she was partly to blame because she'd consciously chosen to let Rafael see the MacDonalds as part of his outpatient list but he'd had no right to push her out of being involved with Angus MacDonald's first surgery. He'd actually told them she was *unavailable*?

Abbie scrubbed harder. It had been a long time since she'd been through this routine and her skin wasn't liking the stiff bristles of the soap-impregnated brush. It stung as she spread her fingers and scrubbed between them and then moved on to the backs of her hands and the insides of her wrists but she didn't lighten the pressure. The physical pain was an echo of the simmering anger she was prodding.

Rafael had been unprofessional. What had stopped him from popping his head into her office and just asking whether she *wanted* to be involved? He hadn't needed to, though, had he? She'd already told him that it was another case she'd love to do.

Being pushed out like that was also confusing. And hurtful.

Wasn't he the one who was so good at maintaining a professional distance that he could put his own emotions aside to make life and death decisions for his own daughter?

Why didn't that automatically apply to his wife?

Because he hated her *that* much now? So much that his desire to avoid working closely with her was enough to make cracks appear in that ability to distance himself?

So much for thinking that they might be able to repair their marriage.

It was proving difficult enough to repair a professional relationship.

Not that others seemed to see that. The nurse who was waiting with a sterile towel held in a pair of tongs was smiling.

'It's so good that you and Mr de Luca are going to be working together again. Everybody's really excited about it.'

Not everybody, Abbie thought grimly. But she smiled back as she took the towel to dry her hands.

'It's been a long time, hasn't it?'

'It's never quite the same without you. Nobody else can work with Mr de Luca like you can. He gets quite cross sometimes.'

Abbie's eyebrows rose as she pulled on her gown and then turned so that the nurse could tie it.

It made her feel a little better to know that no one else could partner Rafael in Theatre as well as she could but it wasn't really a surprise, was it?

Their professional relationship had been astonishingly good from the moment they'd first shared an operating theatre together nearly two years ago.

Had any two surgeons ever clicked like that from the get-go? Complemented each other so perfectly it was as if one surgeon had suddenly doubled their skill set. And not only that. They worked in such a similar way that they could anticipate what the other was thinking or about to do. A silent form of communication and co-operation that had quickly become a talking point in their professional circle.

They'd been dubbed the 'dream team.'

And they'd loved that.

But that had been then. The nurse's comment had been a boost but she'd disappeared with an armful of dirty linen back into the changing rooms, and without her enthusiastic support the thought of working side by side with Rafael in Theatre was enough to make Abbie's heart race and her mouth feel dry.

'Get a grip,' she ordered herself sternly, as she pulled on a pair of gloves.

She'd faced far harder things than this in the last few months. She'd had to make decisions and take actions with nothing more than her instinct to guide her at some points. And she'd had to do it firmly and swiftly. Because she'd had to do it alone.

So she could handle this.

Even if she hadn't expected a challenge like this to appear so fast after Ethan's edict that they work together—or face the consequences.

It was only 11:00 p.m. on the same day, for heaven's sake.

A child had been brought in by helicopter for emergency surgery. Unrestrained, the six-year-old had been ejected from a car in a smash. She had multiple injuries, including two broken arms and major facial trauma.

She needed the best surgeons the Lighthouse had to offer.

Abbie was one of them, so that she could deal

with the initial repair of the facial tissues and skin in the hope of a result that wouldn't be too disfiguring in the future.

Rafael was the other surgeon and he would be able to handle anything that Abbie couldn't. Thanks to his experience as a general paediatric surgeon before he'd specialised first in oncology and then in reconstructive surgery, there was nothing that could happen in an operating theatre that he couldn't manage, at least in an emergency situation.

Knowing that had always made her feel safe. Confident.

All she needed to do now was to tap back into that background confidence. And remind herself of just what she'd achieved with Ella's treatment without that umbrella Rafael could provide.

She could do this. Even if Rafael *didn't* really want her in there.

Taking a deep breath and pressing her lips together in a grimly determined line, Abbie crossed her arms in front of her body and turned so that she could use her back to bump open the swinging doors that led into the brightly lit operating room.

Rafael saw Abbie enter the theatre from the scrub room, holding her gloved hands crossed in front of her body, with only her eyes visible between the bottom of her hat and the top of her mask. He watched only until her gaze met his. He held the eye contact for a heartbeat and then nodded once, turning back to the task ahead. It was a simple gesture but one that had become significant to them both in the past. It conveyed satisfaction. Gratitude. Confidence. There was a difficult job to be done. He needed her to be here. She had arrived.

Things were as good as they could be for the moment.

Had he really thought it would be better if they tried to keep their professional lives as separate as their personal lives had become? At least until things had settled down? Thank goodness Ethan and Leo had taken them both to task and made it a professional duty to start working closely together again or it could have been a very long time before he'd had the bonus of having Abbie by his side like this again.

And he did need her. Rafael had been shocked when he'd met the helicopter crew in the emergency department as they'd transferred the care of little Lucy to his team. She'd been stabilised as far as possible in the rural area where the accident had occurred but there were bigger challenges ahead. The first had been dealt with in the emergency department with the help of a specialist paediatric anaesthetist. Securing a definitive airway had been extremely difficult due to the level of facial trauma but at least it had given him time to get used to the horrific injuries. He just wished he'd had more time to warn Abbie before she arrived in Theatre.

'Oh, my God...' He could hear the way Abbie's breath caught in her throat as she whispered her first reaction.

'It's actually not as bad as it looks,' he told her quietly. 'The jaw's broken in three places and she's lost several teeth. Cheekbones are both fractured and displaced. As is the nose. One ear has been partially amputated but there's no skull fracture or brain haemorrhage. And I think her eyes are okay. It will be easier to see what other damage there is when we get these parts of her face back where they should be. It's the soft-tissue damage that's making things look so bad. The scans are up over there if you want to have a look.'

'Is there a photograph available?' Abbie's initial shock had worn off commendably fast. 'Of what she used to look like?'

'Yes. The grandmother emailed one through. It's been printed out and is beside the viewing screens.'

'Thanks.' Still holding her crossed arms carefully in front of her to avoid any potential contamination and need to rescrub, Abbie moved to examine the images of both the damage and what the little girl's face should look like. It was several minutes before she came back to the table but that was fine. Rafael had a lot of work to do before there would be an area ready for Abbie's delicate touch in repairing delicate vessels and skin tears.

And he needed to concentrate. It wasn't easy, trying to manoeuvre tiny titanium rings into position to try and fix fractured bones back together.

'What's been said about her arms?'

'Colles' fracture on the left. Spiral fracture of the radius and ulna on the right. Looks like she put her arms out to break the fall and then hit the ground face first. Not pretty but it may have saved her from a bad head injury or internal damage.'

'What's been done for them?'

'The arms?' Rafael didn't need this distraction. 'Just support with back slabs until orthopaedics can come in. It's well down the list of priorities.'

'Do we have the X-rays?'

'They're on digital file. Why?' Rafael needed Abbie to focus on what was more of a concern right now—putting this little's girl's face back together.

'Look at this.'

'I can't.' Rafael was waiting for his senior theatre nurse to suck blood away so that he could see where to place the ring he was holding in his forceps. 'I could use some help here, Abbie.'

But Abbie ignored him. 'Scalpel, thanks,' she ordered a registrar. 'And someone throw some antiseptic on this arm.'

Rafael gave up on the ring and looked up, incredulous. 'What are you *doing*?'

'Opening this arm.' Sure enough, Abbie waited only until a nurse had hurriedly swabbed the skin of a small forearm and then she was slicing into it with her scalpel. Rafael's jaw dropped. He'd never seen her act like this.

Ever.

Seconds later, Abbie dropped the scalpel, having left a long, deep incision in the small arm.

She reached for the hand still lying on the table and pressed one of the small fingernails.

'Capillary refill's slow but at least it's there now.'

'It wasn't there before?' Rafael was frowning now. This was the child's right hand, which many might consider even more important to her future quality of life than how her face looked. Had there been a major problem with circulation that had been missed due to his focus on her face? Yes. He could see the unhealthy dark colour the fingers still had. How puffy they were.

'You can still see the swelling in her arm. The fingers were cold and blue. There was no radial pulse.'

'Compartment syndrome...' Rafael took a deep breath. That was why Abbie had incised the muscle casing so decisively. If she hadn't, the result could have been catastrophic. Lucy might have lost her whole hand, let alone the efficient use of it. 'Thank goodness you noticed.'

'If it had started when she was conscious, the

pain level would have alerted someone.' Abbie's gaze was in no way accusing. 'It's just lucky I came in late and wanted an overall picture before getting focussed.'

Rafael could only nod. This was not the time or place to tell Abbie that he was proud of her picking up on the complication. And taking control without waiting for his opinion.

Getting that overall impression was a characteristic that Abbie had much more noticeably than he did these days. She was always fastidious in gathering every piece of information she could about a case. Looking at a bigger picture that included things like family circumstances and relationships. A way of looking at a case that invariably led to the kind of emotional involvement in a patient that he preferred to avoid when possible. That was why they'd always made such a good team. Two halves of an amazing whole. The 'dream team,' as Ethan had reminded them only today.

But hadn't he always been the unspoken leader of that team?

No longer, by the look of things. Abbie had changed since the last time they'd worked like this together. She'd become more decisive. More authoritative. More…independent? In here, that was a good thing. It would give him a partner he would enjoy working with even more. Out of here? That was another matter entirely. Persuading Abbie to forgive him and give their marriage another chance might be an uphill battle.

'Call Orthopaedics,' she was instructing a nurse. 'We'll need them here sooner rather than later. And someone find a dressing to cover this wound in the meantime, please.' She stepped around the table to stand beside Rafael.

So close that their shoulders were touching.

'Now…' Abbie was peering into the area Rafael was working on to align the small jaw again. 'Can I start debriding the cheek tissue? I'd like to get an idea of how much skin we've got left to work with. I suspect we're going to need some grafts.'

Rafael absorbed the feeling of having her this close. He could hear the calm confidence with which she was now assessing the work she had come here to do. Suddenly it was easy to push anything personal and negative into a space that had no relevance in here. He knew without any doubt that within minutes he and Abbie would be working together seamlessly. The way they always had. His own confidence soared. They could do this. Between them they would get the foundation work done that would end up with little Lucy looking as close to the way she'd looked before the accident as was humanly possible.

He hadn't felt this inspired—this *happy* in his work—since...well, since Abbie had left.

How had he not realised how much he'd missed this?

Because he had isolated himself emotionally from his work so effectively?

The way he'd isolated himself from his wife and daughter?

That was in the past. He'd learned his lesson. With the resolution that things were going to change from now on, Rafael didn't dismiss the pleasure of having Abbie working beside him. Instead, he channelled it into making sure he did the best work he was capable of.

Talk about diving into the deep end.

Six hours later, Abbie all but staggered into the changing room where she'd stored her clothes in her old locker. The one beside Rafe's.

She headed for the closest shower, which offered a private area that included a slatted wooden bench seat beneath a hook on which to hang her dry clothes. Having hung what she would change back into on the hook, however, Abbie didn't immediately close the door or turn on the shower to let the water get hot. Instead, she sank down on the wooden seat and closed her eyes for a moment.

Everything ached. Her back and feet seemed to have totally forgotten their ability to stand in one spot for so long without major discomfort. She had cramp in her fingers from the fierce control she had exerted to make every one of the countless sutures she'd made as perfect as possible. Her eyes felt gritty, with a fatigue that was numbing her mind and making it impossible to think of anything but finding the energy to get up and turn on that shower.

And yet Abbie was smiling as she rolled her head in a slow circle, trying to get the painful kinks out of her neck.

How *good* had that been?

Challenging. Intense. But *so* satisfying. She hadn't hidden her skills beneath a deep layer of rust like she'd feared. Even better, she and Rafael had worked together just as they always had. There'd even been at least one of those magic moments when that complete harmony had kicked in and it had felt like it was one surgeon who happened to have four hands.

Finally, Abbie found the strength to stand up and turn on the hot water. She knew it would take at least a minute to heat up, unless they'd made some big improvements in the plumbing while she'd been away, so she stood there waiting and tried rolling her head again because there was one particularly painful spot between her shoulder blades.

'Sore neck?'

The query was accompanied by the metallic scrape of a locker door opening. Rafael must be feeling every bit as exhausted as she was. They'd both gone to Recovery with their small patient to watch over her as her level of consciousness lifted but Rafe had stayed longer, wanting to adjust the level of sedation they would keep her under.

Something stopped Abbie turning around. They had just spent a considerable period of time working so well together. Was it that she didn't want to spoil that by finding that he was avoiding eye contact, perhaps? Or that she might see resentment that would confirm he'd only sent for her because Leo and Ethan had hauled them over the coals about *not* working together?

She put her hand under the stream of water to check the temperature and to excuse her not turning around. 'How's Lucy doing?'

'Very well. When I've had a quick shower, I'll find her grandmother and take her to visit Lucy in Recovery.'

His voice was getting louder with every word. Good grief, had he stepped into this shower cubicle with her? Abbie tensed, ready to turn, but then froze. Apart from the sound of the running water, there was an odd stillness. Maybe Rafe had just gone past the open door to get a towel or something. She might turn and he would be nowhere to be seen and even in the split second when she imagined that possibility, she could also feel the thud of disappointment it would create. But, even as that flitted through her brain, she felt the touch of his hands on her shoulders. His thumbs digging into her spine as they made small circles over her knotted muscles. He knew *exactly* where that sharp ache tended to settle, didn't he?

'Oh...' Abbie let her head droop. 'That feels *amazing...*'

It was by no means the first time she'd been treated to a neck massage after a tough stint in Theatre so it was no surprise he could do it so well. It was, however, the last thing Abbie had expected right now.

What was happening here? The magic she'd wanted when she'd first seen Rafael again and had imagined an embrace that could wipe all out all the grief they'd given each other?

Certainly the sensations Rafael's fingers were conjuring up were enough to wipe out rational thought. Like worrying about any hot water that was being wasted. Tendrils of a pleasure-pain mix were shooting down her spine and arcing right through her body.

But it was just a neck massage. If they hadn't happened to be standing in a shower cubicle it was something that could be perfectly accept-able between any colleagues who were friends and understood the aftermath of the physical challenge they'd just shared. If she started think-ing it was intended to be intimate she could well be lining herself up for disappointment.

'Thanks.' Abbie's movement was subtle but the touch of Rafael's hand vanished instantly. She could feel him taking a step back even as she turned her head to smile at him.

'We did it,' she said.

'Indeed.' Rafael had one hand on the door. He raised his other hand to rub his own neck. 'I'm sure Ethan and Leo will be delighted to hear how well we managed to work together.'

Oh, yes…that disappointment had only been waiting to hit Abbie hard enough to make her lose her emotional footing.

'That wasn't what I meant,' she muttered.

Rafael leaned closer to hear her. Was it inten-tional that the movement pushed the door closed behind him? 'What *did* you mean?'

'That we put Lucy back together. I…I think she's going to get a good result.' Sudden, unwelcome tears stung the back of her eyes. Abbie turned them towards the shower so that Rafael wouldn't see. There was steam billowing out over the top of the curtain now. At least she'd be able to have a good cry when she was under that stream of water. She needed Rafe to go away. Now.

But he didn't. 'We certainly did,' he said. 'And what's more, you probably saved her hand, Abbie. Well done, you.'

The praise was sweet. So sweet that Abbie couldn't hold back the tears now. She had to swipe at them with her hand.

'Oh…Abbie…*cara*…'

Rafe was turning her to face him. Tilting her face up with gentle pressure under her chin. The warmth of the steam around them had nothing on what was sparking between them and had it dampened the oxygen level as well? Abbie's lips parted as she tried to find a new breath.

The caring tone of the endearment Rafael had used still hung between them and it made the flicker of desire in his eyes totally irresistible. Abbie couldn't look away. Her fatigue was forgotten as her body strained towards his, her mind willing him to touch her. To *kiss* her.

She had no idea who moved first, and what did it matter?

This was no gentle reunion kind of kiss. It was how Abbie had dreamed it might be. An incandescent moment that would burn everything else into oblivion. A leap straight back into the fierce passion they had discovered the first time they'd touched each other. A passion that had only grown more powerful the more they'd learned about each other's bodies.

He knew exactly what took her over the edge. The slide of his tongue against the inside of her lip and the way it tangled with the very tip of hers. The slide of his hands inside her clothing and the way those strong hands cupped her buttocks and pulled her against that hardness she knew so well. Wanted so badly…

But somehow it didn't feel right. Maybe it was becoming aware of the splash of water beside them and remembering where they were and how inappropriate this was.

Or…maybe it was something much bigger than that.

In the same way that she had seen the massage as being nothing more than a physical action, a part of Abbie's brain could see that this was only sex.

Passionate, exciting, mind-blowing sex certainly. The kind that had sealed their initial relationship and had led to Ella's conception and had had them rushing headlong into marriage and a lifetime commitment, in fact. A kind that had been enough to keep them sane during the terrible times they'd been through in the course of Ella's illness but, at the end of the day, it was just that. Sex.

And perhaps that wasn't enough any more and that was what didn't feel right.

It was Abbie whose hands stopped moving and touching. Whose lips stilled. Who wriggled free of the intimate contact of their lower bodies.

'We can't do this,' she gasped.

Rafael's gaze slid towards the shower and he sighed. 'Come home with me, then.'

'No.' Abbie shook her head. 'I don't just mean we can't do it *here.*'

There was bewilderment in his gaze now. He had no idea why Abbie had pulled away.

'Can't you see? It's not going to solve anything, Rafe.'

He still didn't understand. And he didn't believe her. He thought he was being rejected and at the flicker of pain—anger, even—Abbie's heart sank. She was doing it again, wasn't she? Attacking his pride. The surest route to strengthening the barrier between them instead of starting to dismantle it.

But she could also see the internal struggle going on. The effort he was making.

His voice was raw. 'Then what is going to solve it, Abbie? *Tell* me.'

There was nothing Abbie wanted more than to tell him.

If only she *knew*.

Rafael waited for a heartbeat. And then another. And then, muttering something in Italian that was probably a curse, he turned and left.

A second later, Abbie heard the bang of a locker door. And then the thump of the changing-room doors being pushed open. Rafael was going somewhere else to shower and who could blame him?

What had she done?

Blown the best chance she could have had to reconnect with the man she loved?

The fatigue came back in a wave that made it unbelievably hard to get on with what she had to do. The feel of her own hands on her skin as she pulled off the scrubs only reminded Abbie of the touch of Rafael's hands and made her feel worse.

What *had* she been thinking?

There was very little traffic around at this time of day, which was just as well because Rafael wasn't paying much attention as he gunned his car in the direction of the only safe place he could think of. His home.

Abbie didn't want him.

Her body did, that much had been obvious, but her heart didn't and that was what mattered.

How the hell could he let her know how much he still loved her if he wasn't allowed to touch her? To let his *body* say the things that were too hard to put into words?

She was being unfair. Shutting them both out of the one area of their relationship they'd never had any problems with. Making sure the spotlight was shining onto the battleground that the rest of their relationship had become.

Why?

The slap of his open hand on the steering-wheel was hard enough to be painful but it didn't shut up the annoying voice in the back of his head. Beneath the burning frustration and the simmering anger it was still there—the faint but insistent message that suggested Abbie was right. That reconnecting sexually would only push the destructive differences under a carpet. That it wouldn't *solve* anything.

But she couldn't even tell him what would.

The way he slammed the car door shut probably woke up several neighbours but Rafael didn't care.

Maybe neither of them knew.

Because the solution didn't exist.

CHAPTER FIVE

'MUM-MUM-MUM…'

Ella was standing in her cot and she flung her arms into the air when her mother entered the room.

'Hey, baby girl…' Abbie reached into the cot and gathered Ella into her arms, careful as always not to tangle the IV line. 'How are you? I've hardly seen you *all* day and I've missed you *so* much.'

'Mum-mum-mum…' Ella's tiny hands were busy, touching Abbie's hair and then her face. And then she rubbed her nose on Abbie's collarbone and made a grizzling sound. Abbie's gaze flew to Melanie, the nurse who was moving to straighten the cot.

'She's just hungry. I was waiting to give her

her bottle in case you made it back in time. I'll go and heat it up now.'

'Thanks, Mel. So she's been okay today?'

'Good as gold. They had a good chat about her on ward rounds. Everybody's very excited about her being such a success story. I think there's a bit of competition over who's going to write up the case history and get it published in a journal.'

'They might have to compete with the guys in New York for that.'

Melanie smiled. 'I'm staying out of it. Bottom line was they only came in to brighten their day, I think. Nothing like a wee miracle like our Ella to make everybody feel better about life in general and work in particular.'

'Mmm.' Abbie cuddled her daughter, rocking her gently. Ella had put her thumb into her mouth and the vigorous sucking noises made both women smile.

'She's starving.' Melanie had picked up the huge teddy bear taking up half the cot, obviously planning to move it out of the way for the night.

The thumb came out of Ella's mouth with a popping noise. *'No-o-o-o...'*

Abbie could feel the small body tensing in her arms. Small lungs expanding to let rip with an uncharacteristic wail.

'Don't take it away,' she told Melanie. 'She's in love.'

'But it's so massive. It takes up most of the cot.'

Abbie's smile was rueful. 'It's pink. And it sparkles. And it was a present from Daddy.'

A somewhat loaded silence fell as Melanie put the tutu-clad bear back into the cot.

'Has...has Rafe been in today?'

'Twice.' Melanie nodded. 'You were visiting Lucy the first time and he was here for a bit this afternoon when you were in Theatre. He asked what time she got her bedtime bottle and said he'd try and get back.' She chewed her lip and the glance at Abbie suggested there was something she was debating whether to say.

Abbie could guess what it was. Rafael wanted

to be the one to give Ella her bottle and put her to bed.

And that was something she wasn't prepared to give up.

Melanie said nothing as she went away to heat the bottle. Abbie settled herself in the armchair with Ella, trying to ignore the prickle of guilt at her determination not to willingly share the next half hour or so of her life. When Melanie returned Abbie asked the nurse to dim the lights in the room and then suggested that she take a break. She'd call if she needed any assistance getting Ella tucked up for the night later.

Bliss. Abbie adjusted the tilt of the bottle as Ella clutched it with both hands and smiled as her daughter relaxed into her sucking and lifted her gaze to meet her mother's. The pure joy of that eye contact with her precious baby as she sucked on the only bottle she had now was the highlight of her day. Just as good as the early days when she'd been able to breastfeed Ella. It was a time when the love she had for this little person was the only thing that mattered and it was huge enough to push everything else to one side.

During the dark days of being alone with such a sick child, it had been the one thing that had kept Abbie sane and offered hope. On the worst nights, it had only been cuddling her to sleep and now that she was well enough to enjoy her warm milk, the hope was even stronger and this time together something to look forward to even more.

It was *their* time. Surely a reward that she had earned?

Her breath escaped in a long, contented sigh as Ella's eyes flickered shut and then snapped open again in determination to stay awake. She wasn't the only one who treasured this time together. She wished she'd been there for the consultants' ward round today but she could imagine the looks and smiles that had been exchanged. Being with Ella did brighten everyone's day. The heaviness around her own heart was finally lifting, too.

The bottle was almost finished and the dead weight of the baby in her arms suggested that sleep had arrived when the door opened softly. Had the sudden tension of seeing Rafael transferred itself to Ella? The baby stirred and whimpered but then settled again, her mouth now slack around the teat of the bottle.

'Ohh…' Rafael quietly shifted the small upright chair and seated himself by Ella's head. 'I'm too late.'

'She was hungry.' The prickle of guilt came back again and this time it was intensified by the emotional turmoil Abbie had been in ever since she'd rejected Rafael sexually in the changing room yesterday. 'Would you like to hold her for a bit before she goes to bed?'

The question was clearly redundant. Big hands slid over her arms and beneath Ella to transfer the weight. Again, Ella stirred and whimpered but soft Italian words of love soothed her within seconds and then Rafael just sat, his head bowed over his daughter, his arms cradling her as if she were the most precious thing on earth.

Abbie was caught. Half lying in the reclining chair, it would take a huge effort to get up and leave father and daughter alone and it would only disturb the moment. Or maybe that was just an excuse. Maybe what had really captured her was the acute awareness of this man beside her.

The...*longing*.

He must have come straight from a shower because his dark curls were damp and she could actually *feel* the warmth coming from his skin. Could smell the fresh scent of soap and maleness. Abbie's gaze was locked on Rafael's hands as he held Ella. Such strong hands with those long, long fingers and the dusting of dark hair on the top. It had been his hands that had first stirred her attraction to him, hadn't it? When he'd been waving them in the air to illustrate something he had been telling her about a case.

Or had it been his eyes? The way they could hold her like a physical caress?

What would happen if she reached out and touched one of those hands now? If, when he looked up at her, she gave him the silent message that she'd been wrong. That being together again in the most intimate way possible *could* be the answer to dissolving the barrier between them?

It had always worked in the past to solve an argument, hadn't it?

'Do you remember the couch?' The soft words seemed to come from nowhere and Abbie was as surprised as Rafael as his head jerked up.

'Scusi?'

'The couch. The white one.'

The supremely comfortable, feather-stuffed, totally impractical and ridiculously expensive white couch. It had been the week before their wedding and they'd been out shopping for furniture in the euphoria that had followed a successful offer on their new apartment. The same euphoria that had made them view Abbie's unexpected pregnancy as nothing more than a sign that they were meant to be together. For ever.

'Of course I remember. I sit on it every day.'

'Do you remember what happened when we found it in the shop?'

Rafael seemed to be ignoring her. He rocked Ella and pressed a gentle kiss to her head. And then he sighed and gave one of those eloquent shrugs.

'So it was our first fight. What of it? What is the point of remembering it now?

'Because...'

Because it was important, even though Abbie wasn't quite sure why.

'Do you remember what you told me? About your parents? About them never arguing?'

'It was true. They didn't.'

'Because your mother did whatever your father ordered to keep the peace. You said it was the Italian way and the husband was the head of the household and his word was law and arguing was a sign of disrespect. And I said it was the

Victorian way and it wasn't going to work for us because I deserved just as much respect, and if it dented your Italian pride then you'd have to suck it up and get over it.'

A snort escaped Rafael. 'I remember. How could I forget?'

'And what did you do then?'

Something rueful tugged at one corner of his mouth. 'I gave you an order.'

'Mmm.'

He had 'ordered' her into bed. It had been a joke, accompanied by a kiss that had demonstrated the kind of passion Abbie knew would take her straight to paradise. The argument about the couch had suddenly become irrelevant and Rafael's pride had been soothed.

And they'd bought the damned couch. A week after it had been installed in the apartment Rafael had spilt a glass of red wine on it and the ugly stain was irreparable. Abbie had gone out and purchased a large, blue throw to cover it. A throw in the colour of the couch *she* had wanted to buy in the first place.

'It was a couch,' Rafael growled. 'A stupid piece of furniture. We could buy another one tomorrow if it mattered.'

'It's not the couch that matters.'

Abbie suddenly realised why she'd dredged up such an ancient disagreement. The reason they'd fought in the first place had just been a practice run for the fight they would have over Ella's treatment. Rafael's pride getting in the way of any kind of compromise had led to the awful ultimatum about the future of their marriage. 'It's the way we resolved the fight we had *about* the couch.'

Rafael's glare told Abbie just how much she *had* hurt him yesterday. But there was something else there, too. Confusion? That was understandable.

'The stain's still there, Rafe,' Abbie said softly. 'It just got covered up.'

He shook his head and muttered something incomprehensible in Italian.

'The reason we fought is still there, too. We never talked about it again, did we? We never tried to resolve anything by talking about it. We just...went to bed.'

'And it *worked*,' Rafael said fiercely. 'It was where we could show each other how much we loved each other.'

'It didn't work when it was really important. When it was about Ella.'

Rafael was silent. He looked down at the sleeping baby in his arms. Abbie could only watch and wait. And hope, desperately, that she had managed to convey at least a part of how important this seemed to her.

But maybe she hadn't.

'It's time Fiorella was in her bed.' Rafael stood up, careful not to disturb Ella. He carried her to the cot and put her down, checking that her IV line and the pump attached to it was still intact and functioning. He tucked Ears in the crook of one arm and then drew the blanket over the small body. Then he reached to pick up the over-sized bear at the foot of the cot.

'Don't take it out,' Abbie said. 'She'll cry if it's not there when she wakes up.'

Rafael looked over at her, his eyebrows raised.

'She adores it. Especially the sparkles.'

Abbie smiled. Rafael smiled back at her.

'Thank you,' she said then.

'What for?'

'Talking to me.' If nothing else, Abbie was beginning to see what the real barrier between them was. It had been there all along, hadn't it? They just hadn't paid any attention to it until it had been too late.

She saw Rafael taking a slow, inward breath. He held her gaze. 'Maybe,' he said slowly, 'we should talk some more.' A corner of his mouth twitched. 'Instead of going to bed?'

Abbie tried to smile but her lips wobbled. 'I'd like that.'

Rafael stepped closer. 'I could take you out.

For dinner…or a coffee. We…we could go to that place you love in the park. The…what's it called? The Moo Cow?'

They'd been around a baby for long enough to change the way they thought and spoke, hadn't they? Abbie smiled again. 'The Cow and Coffee Bean.'

In Regent's Park. The buffer between their home and the clinic, it had always been perfect as an escape for some exercise and fresh air.

'Like…like a date?'

He inclined his head. '*Si*. Like a date.'

Like starting again, even? Maybe this was exactly what they needed. Swept along in the whirlwind of passion that had defined their early relationship and both so committed to their careers, had they ever stayed out of bed long enough when they'd been together to really get to know each other?

She could smile now. 'I'd love that, Rafe. Coffee. And a walk. It would be perfect.'

Perfect for what? A first date? A new beginning?

'It's Saturday tomorrow. I'm sure we can both find a suitable time to be together.'

Abbie held his gaze. Was it too much to hope that that was what they both wanted out of this? To be really *together* again?

'I'm sure we can.'

His nod was satisfied. Rafael touched his fingers to the top of Ella's head in farewell and then stepped away from the cot. For a heartbeat he looked as if he was going to step towards Abbie's chair. As if he wanted to kiss her goodnight. But she could see the way he paused just long enough to think about it and then controlled himself. How hard he was trying when he simply smiled and left.

Fickle spring weather decided to turn on a stunning April day on Saturday.

It felt as though fate was on his side as Rafael waited at the agreed meeting point at the start of the Broad Walk, just beside the zoo. The shriek of overexcited monkeys somewhere was having

the opposite effect, however. Almost like mani-
acal laughter that was taunting him and setting
his nerves on edge.

Did he really think that a pleasant walk on a
sunny day was going to be enough to win Abbie
back?

And what were they going to talk about? *Dio*...
but women loved to talk, didn't they? To pick
things apart and give them far more importance
than they deserved to have. Far more power that
could be so destructive.

Even a few words could destroy things. And
once they were uttered there was no way you
could ever take them back.

*If you take Ella away to do this then our mar-
riage is over.*

Rafael pushed his fingers through his hair. He
wished he had never uttered those fateful words.
He wished Abbie had just let him take her to bed
where he knew he could have put things right.
He wished those damned monkeys would just

shut *up* for a minute. Why wasn't Abbie here yet? Had she changed her mind about this date?

His breath came out in a whoosh of relief as a black cab swooped into the kerb and Abbie climbed out. She was wearing a blue dress he'd never seen before, with no sleeves and a tight bodice and a swirling skirt that reached almost to her ankles above sandal-clad feet. Her hair was loose and shone like a halo in the sunshine and she had a cardigan draped over the arm that held a straw bag and made it look as if she was off to a picnic.

She looked…like the woman he loved. A beautiful, English rose. With that illusion of fragility that was so sexy when you discovered the steely determination and passion that lay beneath.

'Abbie…*salve, cara*. You look *cosi bella*.'

'Thanks.'

Abbie felt strangely shy. As if this really was a 'date.' A time to meet someone who was virtually a stranger to explore what you had in common with them and whether it might be enough to build a future on together. The mix of hope, excitement and physical attraction felt like a flock of butterflies in her stomach. She hadn't felt like this since…well, since her first date with Rafael.

'You…look pretty good yourself, Rafe.'

What an understatement. Old, soft, faded jeans and a black T-shirt. That leather jacket that was also so old it was nearly as soft as the jeans. Rafael pushed the sleeves up a little further, which made his look more casual. And definitely sexier. But his expression dismissed the compliment.

'In these old jeans? I think not.'

Rafael suppressed the urge to take Abbie's hand but couldn't identify what it was that held him back. A sense of Abbie being as tense as he was perhaps?

'Let's get away from here,' he said. 'These monkeys are driving me *pazzo.*'

Abbie's laugh sounded a little forced to her own ears but some of the tension evaporated.

'They are noisy today, aren't they? Can you still hear them from home sometimes?'

She could remember the first time they'd heard unusual sounds coming from the direction of the zoo. Guessing what could be making the sound had become a game as they'd stood in their garden or taken an evening walk down by the canal. Was that an elephant? Or a lion?

Sometimes Rafael would try and imitate the sound until Abbie laughed so hard he would pretend to take great offence and she'd have to soothe his pride. And that had never been difficult. She only had to tell him how wonderful she thought he was, even if he couldn't make an elephant noise to save himself. She only had to distract him with a kiss or two.

Happy times.

For a moment, Abbie was sure Rafael was thinking about the same thing. But then a shadow passed over his face and he shrugged.

'I wouldn't know. I don't seem to spend that much time there these days.' Rafael could see the flash of disappointment in Abbie's eyes. Had he made it sound like he didn't want to be in their home any more? 'Work's been so busy, you know?'

'Mmm. Ethan told me how hard you've been working while I was away.'

While she'd been away. There it was again. The huge thing that lay between them that Rafael had no idea how to make go away. Was talking about it really going to help?

They weren't even talking now. Just walking side by side in silence amongst the throng of Londoners out to enjoy a Saturday afternoon in the sunshine. Trees were vibrant with the fresh, new green of leaves just beginning to unfurl for the new season. Ancient trunks had skirts of bluebells and daffodils. There were young mothers pushing prams, a father giving a toddler a ride on his shoulders, small children on bicycles and tricycles, teenagers weaving with dangerous speed through the pedestrians on their skateboards...

'Mind out!' Rafael's arm was around Abbie's shoulders in a flash, guiding her out of the path of a speeding youth. The feel of the bare skin of her shoulder beneath his hand was a jolt of sensation that arrowed through his entire body. Hastily, he dropped the contact. Abbie didn't want this, did she?

Oddly, the touch of Rafael's hand on her bare shoulder had felt less intimate than his automatic instinct to protect her. And it had felt…wonderful. She might have had to stand completely on her own feet for the last few months and become stronger because of it but it didn't mean that she didn't want to feel cherished.

Loved.

The speed with which he dropped the contact was disappointing. Abbie bit her lip, trying to think of something to say.

'Do you think it will be this crowded in the coffee shop?'

'I expect so.' Rafael could feel himself scowling. If they couldn't talk to each other in the relative privacy of being outside, what was it going to be like in the café? Would they sit in silence and sip their lattes amidst the buzz of the conversation of others? With the tension between them steadily increasing?

'I know.' Abbie tilted her head, peering past people to see where they were exactly. 'Let's get coffee to go from the cart over there and take it to the Secret Garden. That's always quieter.'

It didn't take long because they knew the route so well. Off the Inner Circle and through the large circular garden with the statue of Hylas in the pond. You could see the imposing structure of St John's Lodge from here, reputedly owned by the Sultan of Brunei these days. But they weren't after an imposing view.

Rafael led the way on a wide grass path, past the blossoms of the dog roses and the twisted trees of white wisteria. Beneath a leafy arbour to the circle of lime trees around a stone urn. And...*yes*...the covered seat at one end of the garden was unoccupied at the moment.

For a moment, Abbie lost all sense of time. She wasn't here with her estranged husband, trying to find a way to reconnect. She was here with the man she was head over heels in love with. Wondering why he was leading to her such a secluded, *romantic* spot. Why the destination seemed so important, the mission so urgent.

And then the reality of the difference this time kicked in and Abbie's step faltered. It was an audible effort to catch her breath.

Rafael almost groaned aloud when he sensed Abbie's step faltering. What had he been thinking in following this particular route? He had led Abbie back to the exact spot he'd proposed to her.

Closing his eyes for a heartbeat, Rafael cursed himself for his insensitivity and wondered how he could rescue the situation, but then he heard Abbie take a deep breath.

'Perfect,' she murmured.

Rafael's eyes flew open. 'It is?'

'Mmm.' Abbie offered him a smile that was

almost shy. 'If we're going to start again, what better place than back where it all started?'

They were going to start again? There was *hope*? And he'd chosen the perfect place? Rafael could feel his chest expand just a little. This time he didn't suppress the urge to take Abbie's hand and he didn't let go until they were seated side by side on the small bench. They could see people through the arbour but, for the moment, they had this small patch of the park to themselves.

'So...' Rafael cleared his throat. He was ready to face whatever was coming even if his heart did seem to be beating faster than usual. 'What shall we talk about?'

Abbie closed her eyes for a moment. What did he think they needed to talk about? The weather? The thought almost made her smile because that was exactly what they'd talked about the last time they'd sat on this bench. They'd actually had to brush snow away before they'd sat down and she'd been freezing and Rafael had opened his coat and tucked her in beside him. He wanted to keep her warm, he'd said. To look after her. For ever.

She opened her eyes but didn't look up at Rafael.

'Us,' she said quietly. 'That's what we need to talk about.'

Oh, no… Rafael drained the last of his coffee. This was worse than he'd feared. Abbie wanted to analyse their relationship and pick it apart. His voice came out more harshly than he had intended. 'What about us?'

Abbie met his gaze. There was a tiny frown line above her eyes. 'Well…we don't really know each other, do we?'

'Pfff…' Rafael couldn't help the incredulous sound. Or the movement of his hands, one of which slashed through the air while the other crushed the empty paper cup it was holding and dropped it on the bench beside him. It was an effort not to jump to his feet as the words tried to rush past each other to get out.

'Of course we know each other. We're *married*. We...' *Love each other?* No. He couldn't speak for Abbie. He changed tack. 'I know you, Abbie. I know that you like two sugars in your coffee. That you hate lacy knickers because they make you itch. That people who hurt their children make you very, very angry.' He was counting off his list on his fingers. 'That one of your favourite surgeries is making new little ears for children. That—'

But Abbie was shaking her head as she set her own cup carefully aside. 'I mean something that goes deeper than that. You don't know *why* I did what I did. Why I had to take Ella to New York even if it was going to mean the end of the marriage that meant so much to me.'

'But I do...' Rafael swallowed hard. 'I know that your little sister, Sophie, died when you were only twelve. That you felt your parents had failed her because they refused to try any treatment that might have added to her suffering when they knew it would gain nothing but a little more time. But that was different. It wasn't leukaemia and *we* tried everything we could even it *was* only going to give us a little more time. The idea that the treatment in New York could really work was…'

Way too much of a miracle to hope for. Rafael's words trailed into silence. It had worked, hadn't it? He'd been wrong.

'You knew the reason,' Abbie agreed quietly. 'But you didn't understand how I *felt* about it because if you had you would have been there with me, Rafe. By my side. And it really hurt that you weren't.'

It hurt thinking about Sophie, too. The little sister she'd lost. The way her family had fallen apart. Sophie had been ill for so long that family life had centred exclusively on her and Abbie had felt almost invisible. The feeling had only strengthened after her sister's death. Had her parents been too afraid to love her too much in case they lost her, too? Did they come to blame each other—the way she secretly did—for not having tried hard enough to save Sophie?

Or did all the love just die because it got smothered under the grief?

She'd tried so hard....

She'd been driven to fight for Ella instead of standing back and watching her die. But her new family had still fallen apart, hadn't it? Was it impossible to win in a dreadful situation like that?

Rafael could see the pain he'd caused by reminding Abbie of what she'd lost as a child. And by not being there for her in New York when she'd needed him. What could he say?

'I'm sorry.' The words were raw. 'I was wrong.'

This time it was Abbie who took hold of his hand. 'It's not just your fault, Rafe. Don't you see? I couldn't understand why you were so opposed to it, any more than you could understand me. Oh, I knew how much you hated to see children suffering when there couldn't be a positive outcome, and that's why you changed specialties to get away from oncology, but this was your own daughter. I just didn't get it.' She bit her lip. 'We don't get each other.'

'Get?' Sometimes, if he was really fired up about something, his languages could tangle in his head and make him miss subtleties.

'Understand. No…it's more than that, I think. If you really love someone and you can understand *why* they feel the way they do, then you'll support them, even if you might not agree with whatever it is.'

Rafael turned the words over in his head. 'You're right,' he said into the quietness. 'I should have supported you.'

'And maybe I should have supported *you*.'

'*Che cosa*? But I was wrong. You only have to look at Ella to see that I was wrong.'

'But if I'd understood *why*, maybe we could have changed things. All I could see was someone who was being a doctor, not a father. Or a husband. Someone who couldn't *feel* what I was feeling.'

It was true. He had isolated himself emotionally. Circumstances had then isolated him physically.

But they were closer now, surely? They were talking about things they'd never talked about before.

'It won't happen again,' he told Abbie. 'I love you. I love Ella. I want to be a good father and husband.' He touched her face. Cupping it gently the way he always had before trying to convey his sincerity with a tender kiss.

But Abbie pulled away from his touch. 'Don't,' she whispered. 'Please, don't.'

It was too bittersweet, that touch. She could give in to it so easily but it still wouldn't solve anything. It would still be a throw covering a stain.

Rafael dropped his hand. He turned to stare straight ahead and Abbie followed his line of vision. Through the arbour she could see a young couple, wrapped in each other's arms, sharing a passionate kiss. As intent on each other as Abbie and Rafael had been when they'd first come here together. As oblivious to the twists of fate that might pull them apart in the future.

Rafael had to turn away from the sight of the young lovers. He and Abbie had been that close once. He'd hoped that they might get that close again today but they were as far apart as they had been before they had come here, weren't they? Talking had solved nothing.

'I'm still hurting, Rafe.' Abbie spoke so quietly he had to strain to hear the words. 'And I can't go through anything like this again. I know Ella needs her father as much as she needs her mother right now but…I need time. I need to be sure.'

Rafael closed his eyes. She wasn't the only one who was still hurting. 'And how did you think it made me feel, Abbie? When you wouldn't listen to anything I had to say? When you took Ella away and I was so sure I would never see her again? Never hold her? You're not the only one who was hurt.'

'I know. And I'm sorry.'

Rafael's fingers found a tangled part of his hair but he shoved them through the obstruction, welcoming the pain. 'Can we ever get past this? What do we do now?'

'I hope we can get past this.' But Abbie's smile was shaky. Unsure? 'And now? I think we should go and spend some time with our daughter.'

It was Abbie who picked up the empty coffee cups and found a rubbish bin to put them in. She put on the soft cardigan she'd been carrying because there were a few clouds in the sky now and when the sunlight dimmed, the temperature dropped noticeably. The picnic feel to the day was gone. The date was over. They walked out of the Secret Garden and back through the main park in silence but it was a different kind of silence from the one when they'd first entered the park together.

Things were out in the open. Yes, their marriage was still on the line but it seemed that they both *wanted* to repair it, at least. Surely that was a good thing?

'Maybe, one day soon,' he said, 'we'll be able to bring Ella to the park. To show her the Secret Garden.'

'I hope so,' Abbie responded. 'And we could take her to the zoo.'

'To see the monkeys.' The unenthusiastic tone made them both look at each other. And then they both smiled.

She understood. And if they did go to the zoo, she would know that it was a generous act on his part because those monkeys drove him *pazzo*.

He could feel his heart lift. The connection was there. And the love. Surely it was going to be possible to build a bridge over the troubled waters that still lay between them?

It had to be possible, Rafael decided as they went through the ornate iron gates and he raised his arm to flag down a taxi.

It was as simple as that, really.

CHAPTER SIX

GIFTS WERE STARTING to pile up in Ella's room.

While the big pink bear was the frontrunner in the popularity stakes, everybody who looked after Ella was enjoying the growing stack of bright picture books and the toys, especially the board with the animal pictures and the buttons that made the appropriate noise for the animal when Ella pushed it. Her attempts to imitate the noises made them all laugh.

And Rafael had a new audience on which to try out his own animal noises.

'This is a lion, Ella. *Rrrroahhh…* You'll hear them when we take you to the zoo one day. You might even hear them at home. And this is a monkey. *Eeek, eeek, eeek.'*

The noises made both Ella and Abbie grin but

they had yet to hear their little girl giggle again. What would it take?

'You don't have to bring a present every time you come, Rafe. You're spoiling her.'

'I want her to look forward to seeing me.' But Rafael put the bag he was carrying today on the floor and leaned on the edge of the cot, watching as Abbie caught the small, waving arms and pushed them gently into the sleeves of her sleep suit.

'Mum-mum-mum,' Ella crowed.

'That's me.' Abbie snapped some fastenings closed. 'Mama. Can you say papa?'

Ella stared up at her, her eyes round.

'Papa?' she repeated encouragingly.

Ella grinned. 'Mum-mum-mum.'

'I think that's the only word she knows.' Rafael was also smiling but Abbie could sense his disappointment. She tried to distract him.

'She's pretty good at "no." You should have heard her at lunchtime when I tried to persuade her to eat some carrots.'

'She doesn't like carrots?'

'Not yet. Same with pumpkin.'

'Maybe it's the colour she doesn't like.'

'Hmm… You could be right.' Abbie smiled and caught Rafael's gaze. 'It does clash with pink, doesn't it?'

His answering smile was swift and, for a heartbeat, things felt good. There were more of these moments now, when it felt like there was a real connection between them again. The time they'd spent in the park together had been a good starting point but, even with more time with both of them here with Ella and more moments when they were in tune with each other, that distance between them didn't appear to be shrinking.

Ella was the driving force behind Abbie's motivation for trying to repair her marriage. She desperately wanted her daughter to grow up with a loving father in her life. For them all to make a *real* family. But the connection had to there between her parents, too. It had to be more than physical and it had to be strong enough to last the distance. While they were reaching out tentatively to see if they could find and build on that kind of connection, sadly it was Ella who was making things harder.

Oh, she loved the presents. And she loved seeing her daddy and having a cuddle. As long as she wasn't tired. Or sore. Or hungry. Or had a dirty nappy or anything else that was making life a little less joyful. At those times, she only wanted Abbie.

Mum-mum-mum.

As the days passed it was obvious that Rafael was feeling excluded. It wasn't just an Italian's pride that was being dented. Any father would feel disheartened by the preference that Ella made crystal clear when it was needed. And it wasn't something that Abbie could fix, was it? Rafael hadn't been there for such a long time. A quarter of Ella's life. Was it any wonder that the baby saw him as a visitor in her life? That she expected her mother to provide everything from food to comfort?

Abbie glanced at her watch. Any minute now and the nurse would arrive with Ella's night-time bottle. And Rafael was here. She should let him feed her.

Maybe it was the biggest olive branch she could offer?

She couldn't put it into words but when she picked Ella up and offered her to Rafe as the nurse came in with the bottle of warm milk, she could see that he understood how significant this was. The way his gaze held hers with a flash of surprise and then gratitude and then a flood of warmth that felt like pure love was enough to bring a huge lump to her throat.

Rafael sat down in the armchair with Ella in his arms. She was happy enough to lie there until she caught sight of the bottle. The hungry whimper was followed by her head craning so far sideways Abbie feared for her neck.

'Mum-mum-mum...' Small arms were reaching out for her.

Rafael chased her mouth with the teat of the

bottle but Ella was having none of it. She arched her body into a stiff bow and her face went an alarming shade of red.

Abbie had to force herself not to scoop Ella out of her father's arms. 'Try again,' she said above the noise Ella was starting to make. 'She'll get used to the idea of you feeding her in a minute.'

But Rafael shook his head. 'I can't bear to hear her this unhappy. You do it, Abbie.' He stood up and all but shoved Ella into her arms.

It felt like defeat. Worse, even when Ella settled and started sucking hungrily, the joy of doing this was somehow diminished. Abbie could feel Rafael's gaze on her, and she could feel his despair. And there seemed to be something accusing in the gaze Ella had fixed on her, too. She felt like the meat in a sandwich. All she was trying to do was stick the layers back together. Why was it so difficult?

'I'm sorry,' she said quietly to Rafael.

He gave one of those eloquent shrugs. 'It's not

your fault. Fiorella is a baby. All she knows is what she wants to make her happy.'

But Abbie knew what she wanted to make *her* happy, too. And it seemed as far away as ever.

'I…um…thought I might come home tomorrow. After work.'

Rafael went very still. Oh, help…

'Just to see if I find a suitable dress and shoes and things or whether I'll need to go shopping. For the wedding on Saturday?'

'Ah… Of course.'

'I thought you might like to be here with Ella while I'm gone. If you're free about five o'clock, you could feed her her dinner.'

A faintly incredulous huff escaped Rafael but Abbie ignored it. 'If I'm not here, she might be happy to let you feed her. And food is different from a bottle. She lets nursing staff feed her sometimes. We can only keep trying, can't we?'

A sigh this time. *'Si…'* Rafael's expression was unreadable. 'This is true.'

* * *

'She's doing well, isn't she, Mr de Luca?'

'She certainly is.' Rafael stroked the hair of the little Afghan girl, Anoosheh, and smiled at her. It had been nearly two weeks since her massive surgery and the swelling was going down nicely.

'She's learning English fast,' his registrar put in. 'Can you say hello to Mr de Luca, Anoosheh?'

''Ello,' Anoosheh said obligingly. 'I am 'appy to see you, Dock-a-dor.' The words were an effort to produce and then her face twisted into an odd expression.

'She's trying to smile,' the nurse told them. 'It's still hard.'

'Keep trying,' Rafael told his small patient. 'Soon you will be lighting up the world with your smile.'

They all had to keep trying, didn't they?

Even when it didn't seem to be working.

The parts of his life were all there and, if you took each one on its own, there wasn't anything obvious that was broken.

Work was fine. Little Anoosheh was a triumph and one that was being followed closely enough by the media for Rafael's reputation to be growing rather too fast for his liking. Only this morning he'd had to pass a request to appear on a television talk show over to Ethan—who probably passed it to Declan. Far better that the charity projects of the Hunter Clinic got some good publicity than that he became the poster boy for reconstructive plastic surgery.

Ella was fine, too. Doing better each day. The three-month mark when her bone marrow could be checked again was rapidly approaching and if the results were good, her central line could be removed and she would be allowed home. Even better, his precious daughter was happy and she had no trouble lighting up the world with *her* smile.

There had been no objections when he'd been the one to feed her the other evening and he'd done it again last night because it seemed that Abbie did need a new dress for Leo and Lizzie's upcoming wedding and it had given her a chance to hit the high street.

Yes. The wheels of his life were turning perfectly well.

It was when Rafael's ward rounds took him to visit Lucy, the little girl who'd been in the car crash, that he realised what was bothering him so much.

Lucy's grandmother was beside the bed, holding a drink that Lucy was sipping through a straw. She watched as Rafael checked the chart and then gently examined the little girl's face.

'Can you open your mouth a little for me, chicken? Does that still hurt?'

'Mmm.'

'It will get a little better each day. But only if you keep trying.' Rafael covered her right eye with one hand and then held up his other hand. 'How many fingers can you see?'

'Free.' The word had to come out without her mouth moving.

'Good girl.' Rafael smiled at the grandmother. 'The vision's improving.'

She nodded. 'Mrs de Luca had a specialist from the eye department come in this morning. They think it's going to be fine. And the ortho-paedic surgeon is happy with her arms and the movement she's got in her fingers. Mrs de Luca took some of the stitches out of her face this morning, too. It's looking a bit better, isn't it?'

Rafael could hear the doubt in the woman's voice. 'If you'd seen Lucy when she came into Theatre, you would know that what Mrs de Luca did is just amazing. Lucy will need more sur-gery later but, eventually, I suspect you're going to have to look carefully to see any lasting dam-age.' His reassurance was sincere. The pride he felt in Abbie's work even more heartfelt.

'She's your wife, isn't she? Mrs de Luca?'

'She is.'

In name only, however. The taunting whisper stayed with Rafael as he finished his round of the surgical ward.

The wheels of his life might be turning perfectly well but the cogs weren't fitting together properly so the wheels weren't turning *together*. Was it only coincidence that working together to operate on Lucy had been the only time they'd been that close professionally since she'd returned?

She should be here now, sharing this ward round. Sharing the pleasure in the little girl's excellent progress. But she'd been here before him today and she was in Theatre this afternoon. Creating a new ear for the patient she'd seen on the morning of that first outpatient clinic together. The one that had led to Leo and Ethan ordering them to put their personal issues aside and work together properly again. But they weren't, were they? Even this patient they'd worked so hard on together was now being followed up on at different times.

His time with Ella was wonderful but she would only allow him to do things for her when Abbie wasn't there.

There was nothing wrong with his home either, except that the only time Abbie had gone there had been when he had been *here*, looking after Ella.

How could they possibly put things right when they were beginning to shape their lives into completely separate wheels? It wouldn't matter how smoothly they turned, it wouldn't be any kind of a marriage and he wouldn't blame Abbie for deciding it wasn't good enough.

Somehow he had to get the cogs to fit inside each other. To show Abbie that, by doing so, the 'machine' of them being together would be stronger. Able to do so much more. Could last for ever, like a beautifully crafted clock.

But marriage wasn't a machine, was it? He was thinking about this all the wrong way. And maybe it was that kind of thinking that had caused their problems right from the start.

Waiting by the lift when he'd left his junior staff to follow up on any new orders for his patients, Rafael couldn't shake off the disturbing undercurrent his analogy of timepieces had left him with.

You couldn't divorce emotion from things that happened to people. He was too good at standing back and seeing the big picture without the emotional layers. The way he had when it had come to making that decision about Ella's experimental treatment. Perhaps the way he had when he'd voiced that 'all or nothing' ultimatum about their marriage? When he looked at the big picture, he saw it in terms of benefit versus suffering for the individual involved from a clinical perspective.

Abbie was the opposite. She saw the same big picture, but her scales weighed the emotions of everybody involved and not just the patient at the centre of the decision to be made. And the results she came up with were very different sometimes.

But not *wrong*.

Rafael knew that. He also knew that he'd made things much worse while Abbie and Ella had been away in New York. He'd buried himself in his work and when he had thought about his family, the fear that he would never see his daughter again had been easily shrouded in anger and then resentment towards Abbie. He'd been cool and clipped in any communication. No wonder it had trailed away into impersonal emails and text messages.

But how did you go about changing something that was a part of your personality? How could you learn to feel the things that someone like Abbie could feel?

By finding someone to teach you?

The lift doors slid open in front of him but, instead of stepping in, Rafael turned swiftly and headed for the stairs.

Abbie knew it was Rafael coming into the theatre without even having to turn her head.

What she didn't know was why he had come in. The surgery for the grade-three microtia on seven-year-old Annabelle was well under way.

Rib cartilage had been harvested and Abbie was sculpting the new ear. She had to look up for a second as Rafael stepped closer, however. Had something happened to Ella?

The eye contact was reassuring. 'Don't let me interrupt,' Rafael said. 'I just had the urge to come and watch an artist at work.'

Abbie blinked. 'Really? What brought this on?'

'I was checking Lucy. Admiring your needle-work. And then I remembered you were doing this today and it's been a long time since I've watched the procedure. Do you mind?'

'No, of course not.' Hardly. He had been admiring her work? Wanted to watch 'an artist'? How could anyone object to such a professional accolade?

It put the pressure on a little more, though. Not that Abbie hadn't been doing her best before but now she was determined to make this *perfect*.

'This is Annabelle,' she told Rafael. 'She's been waiting a long time for this surgery but I needed her to be old enough to have sufficient rib cartilage to harvest.'

'She could have had the surgery much younger with a Medpor reconstruction, couldn't she?'

Was Rafael criticising her choice? Abbie couldn't help sounding a little defensive.

'Using an artificial framework means that the ear can't match the other one perfectly. It also doesn't grow with the child. This creates an ear that's alive. One that's going to last a lifetime.'

'But not many surgeons are gifted enough to do it well. Annabelle is lucky to have found you.'

There was a murmur of agreement from the rest of the team. Abbie shook off the praise. 'I think she chose me because I said I'd put an earring in to match her other ear so it'll be there when the bandage comes off for the first time next week.'

Happy with the shape of the outer ear she had carved from the cartilage, Abbie turned her attention to the peanut-shaped deformity that had been Annabelle's right ear until now. She could use the lower part for the ear lobe. The tiny gold stud earring was bathed in disinfectant and waiting in a kidney dish nearby.

Rafael was watching her examination of the deformed ear tissue.

'She must have been teased a lot at school.'

'Yes. She's kept it covered pretty well with her hair but she was very self-conscious about it. Her mother said they had all sorts of problems when she was expected to do swimming at school.'

'Has it affected her badly, do you think?'

'Well, she's very shy. Hard to say whether she would have been more outgoing without the deformity but I'm sure it's contributed. It would have become progressively more of an issue as she got older, of course.'

'*Si*... It would be torture for a teenage girl to look so different.'

'Mmm. That's why I favour the rib graft method. She'll need a bit more surgery to refine things down the track but by the time

Annabelle's interested in boys, her ear will look and feel as if it's always been there.'

This was weird. She might have expected a keen interest from Rafael but Abbie would never have picked that it would focus on the emotional side of the surgery and its aftermath. Why wasn't he asking about the dimensions of the suture material she was using? Or the technique for elevating a skin flap to preserve all the hair follicles so that Annabelle wouldn't be left with a bald patch?

'She has conduction deafness, I assume?'

'Yes. There's no ear canal or eardrum on this side.' That was more like it. A clinical query.

'Is that causing problems for her? Or her family?'

'Doesn't seem to be.' He was doing it again. Looking past the clinical picture and considering the bigger, emotional picture. Something was going on in his head, Abbie realised. He was making a deliberate effort. To connect with her way of thinking about patients, perhaps?

Whatever it was, she liked it.

'They're under the care of an audiologist to make sure they look after the good side.' Abbie was peering through the magnifying lenses she wore to make tiny stitches that attached the ear lobe to the new part she had crafted. 'I think they're all more concerned about the cosmetic side of it all at the moment, though.'

She checked again that the lobe was at exactly the same level as Annabelle's other ear.

'Looking good.' Her registrar nodded. 'You ready for the earring?'

Abbie grinned. 'Let's do it.'

Even when the surgery was completed, the pressure dressing in place and protected with the plastic cup that was taped on, Rafael didn't seem inclined to talk about anything clinical.

'Were you happy with Lucy's progress?'

'She's doing well, isn't she?' Abbie stripped off her mask and gloves. 'I'll be happier when she can eat again, though. She's lost quite a lot of weight.'

'I've arranged for a physiotherapist who specialises in maxillofacial injuries to start working with her. Her grandmother's keen to help, too.'

'It's great that she's got the family support there.' But Abbie sighed as she pulled off her gown. 'Her mother's still in ICU. It's not looking hopeful.'

'And the father?'

'Not in the picture.' Abbie balled up the gown and threw it in the bin. 'Hasn't been since she was a baby.'

A broken family. The kind that Abbie didn't want for Ella. Or for herself or Rafael, for that matter. She forced a smile to her lips.

'On a more positive note, I found a gorgeous dress *and* shoes for the wedding tomorrow. Did you get your suit cleaned?'

'I have to pick it up at the dry-cleaner's after work.'

'But you'll come and see Ella later?'

'Of course.'

The smile was genuine this time. 'We'll look forward to that.'

'Me also. And tomorrow…the wedding? It will be another date for us, perhaps?'

The hopeful expression in Rafael's eyes almost undid Abbie completely. If they weren't still standing in Theatre, with staff busy around them cleaning up after Annabelle had been taken to Recovery, she might have thrown her arms around his neck. Stood on tiptoe to provide reassurance with a kiss.

But all she could do was smile. And offer a quiet word that was only for Rafael.

'Absolutely.'

CHAPTER SEVEN

THE PHOTOGRAPHS OF this wedding would grace the pages of any magazine devoted to the lifestyles of the rich and famous.

As a venue, Claridge's was simply one of the best London could offer. Intimate tables for the wedding breakfast, which seated only three or four people each, could be seen in an adjoining area, draped in white cloth with centrepieces of trios of white roses in simple vases amidst sparkling crystal glasses and gleaming silverware. Larger arrangements of flowers, also white, were dotted everywhere amongst the pillars.

The area that Rafael and Abbie were ushered to be seated was also extremely elegant. There would be many more people arriving for the reception but the ceremony itself was more private and a semicircle of comfortably padded chairs for the guests was arranged beneath a spectacular chandelier, giving everybody a clear view of the sweeping staircase that the bride would come down to make her entrance. The seats were mostly filled by the time Abbie and Rafael edged into the back row. She said hello to Lexi Robbins, Head of PR at the Hunter Clinic. Lexi was holding hands with the man on her other side, surgeon Iain McKenzie, and it was almost palpable how much in love these two were. Neither of them was particularly aware of the existence of anybody else and their private, whispered communication was probably about a different wedding. One that they would be starring in themselves in the not-too-distant future.

It was a very different wedding that Abbie couldn't help thinking about, too. Sitting here, all dressed up, it felt like she and Rafael were in a silent little bubble amongst the other guests. A tense kind of silence. Was he also thinking about the last wedding he had attended?

Their wedding?

The memory of that day was blurry. If it wasn't for the photograph taken on the steps of the registry office and the ring she still wore on her finger, it would be easy to believe that it had never really happened. They'd done it all too fast, hadn't they? It was all rather a blur. Falling in love with Rafael, finding out she was pregnant and then buying the apartment and getting married within just a few weeks.

Would it have all been different if she hadn't been pregnant?

Of course it would.

Would Rafael have even proposed if things had been different?

Abbie stole a sideways glance at him but Rafael's line of vision was firmly fixed elsewhere. As the muted buzz of conversation faded around her, Abbie's head turned as well. Within moments of Lizzie appearing, the only sound around her was the soft classical music of the string quartet in the background. Leo stood near the foot of the staircase with Ethan beside him—Abbie had heard how Lizzie had convinced Ethan to be Leo's best man after he'd originally refused due to their strained relationship—and, like everyone else now, the groom's gaze was fixed on Lizzie as she came slowly down, her bridesmaid several steps behind her.

Her dress was gorgeous. Simple but striking with cap sleeves of the lace that overlaid the rest of the dress and a slim belt with a silver buckle above soft folds of fabric that flowed over the stairs and then grazed the black and white marble of the chequerboard floor. The bouquet she carried was simply a bunch of the same perfect white roses that were the centrepieces on the tables. Leo and Ethan had matching white rosebuds as buttonholes in their classic, dark morning suit jackets over pinstriped grey trousers.

The wedding vows exchanged were traditional. The same words that Rafael and Abbie had said to each other.

*To have and to hold... For better or for worse...
In sickness and in health...*

*To love and to cherish, from this day forward,
until death us do part...*

Maybe the memories of her own wedding day weren't that blurry after all. The words echoed in her head but something strange was happening in the rest of her body. Her heart was back in that registry office. Full to bursting with *so* much love.

So many hopes and dreams for her future with this wonderful man.

Her breath must have caught audibly. Not that anyone else would have noticed Rafael's attention being diverted but his body was suddenly closer. Touching hers. With no conscious thought on her part, Abbie found her hand stealing into Rafael's. Their fingers laced together and the grip was tight enough to know that she wasn't the only one being swamped by emotion.

They had vowed to love each other. In sickness and in health. Did it matter if it was Ella's health rather than either of theirs?

Of course it didn't.

Had they broken their vows? They were still married, weren't they?

Abbie was fighting tears as she watched the tender first kiss of the newlyweds in front of them.

Yes. She and Rafael had broken their vows because they hadn't cherished each other. And the fault was on both sides.

But how could they have given each other what they'd needed when they hadn't really known each other? They had both wanted the best for Ella. Rafael must be feeling so guilty now, thinking that he had been ready to give up, and here she was, defying the odds.

Abbie squeezed his hand more tightly and was grateful for the answering pressure. And then they both turned their heads as the clapping around them started and Abbie could have drowned in the depths she saw in Rafael's eyes.

She couldn't pull her hand free to join in the congratulatory clapping. She couldn't look away from Rafael's gaze either.

This moment took her straight back to their own wedding. To the way Rafael had looked at her in the heartbeat after the celebrant had told him he could kiss his bride.

It was the most natural thing in the world for him to tilt his head towards her now and for Abbie to raise her face.

A soft kiss. Nothing like the explosive release of need that had happened in the changing room. This was tender. Too brief but long enough.

A cherishing kind of kiss…

'You're crying, *cara*.' Rafael studied her face as he raised his head again. He used the pad of his thumb to brush away a tear.

'It's a wedding.' Abbie sniffed and dipped her head, pressing her fingers against the bridge of her nose to force back any more tears. She looked up and tried to smile. 'You're allowed to cry.'

'*Si...*' Rafael was smiling back at her. 'You're lucky we didn't get married in Italy. The whole village might have been crying.'

Abbie snorted softly but the sound was poignant. The registry office had only been supposed to be a first wedding—getting the formal paperwork out of the way—because Abbie hadn't wanted to be a pregnant bride. Rafael had promised he would take her to Italy as soon as the baby could travel and they could do it all again in a village church on his beloved Amalfi Coast. She would have a beautiful dress and their families would be able to share the celebration not only of their union but the start of their family.

Was it another dream that was nothing but dust now? She had to clear her throat. 'Happy crying, I hope.'

'Of course. What else?' But Rafael's gaze had moved. Somebody was turning from a chair in the next row to greet him and conversations were starting again around them as the newlyweds

moved on to sign the register. They would disappear for photographs soon and Abbie knew that
the gathering would become a glittering social
occasion as the wider circle of guests arrived.
There were rumours that royalty was expected,
even, as some of the Hunter brothers' clients had
been invited to share this celebration.

Suddenly Abbie didn't want to be part of it.

She wanted to be alone somewhere.

With her own husband.

Maybe he felt the same way. Maybe that was
why Rafael kept hold of Abbie's hand when they
were free to move around and mingle.

Abbie wasn't complaining.

It felt better than good. It felt right.

There was no shortage of people they knew to
talk to and groups formed as champagne and
canapés were served by an army of waiting
staff. Friends and family of the bride and groom
drifted into one group and the medical person-
nel from the Hunter Clinic, the Lighthouse Chil-

dren's Hospital and Princess Catherine's made up another.

'Abbie…what a gorgeous dress.' The office manager from the clinic, Gwen, was balancing a glass in one hand and what looked like a tiny square of rye bread topped with caviar in the other.

Rafael nodded his approval of the compliment. The new rose-pink dress *was* gorgeous but, in his opinion, it only worked because it made Abbie's skin and hair look irresistibly beautiful. An elegant version of the picnic frock she had worn to the park the other day when she'd taken his breath away.

'Thanks, Gwen. I love your hat, too.' Abbie was eyeing the froth of flowers and feathers on Gwen's head. 'Though it's more of a fascinator, isn't it?'

'A hybrid.' Gwen smiled. 'I believe it's called a "hatinator." Whatever next?' She looked at the canapé her hand. 'This is my second one of these. They're simply delicious.' She glanced from Abbie to Rafael. 'You're not eating?'

'I wanted to hold my wife's hand,' Rafael said solemnly. 'But I couldn't refuse a glass of champagne. What is a man to do?'

He could feel an increase of pressure from the fingers entwined with his. Was Abbie privately expressing her approval of this contact?

He really didn't want to be here, being sociable, any more. He wanted to be alone somewhere.

With Abbie.

Gwen laughed. 'Now, there's an idea. A new kind of diet. You could write a book and become famous.'

'He's already famous.' Another figure joined their conversation. 'I hear that they want to make a movie about transforming the lives of Afghan children and Hollywood is demanding Mr Rafael de Luca as the star.'

The deadpan manner in which this information was delivered made it sound quite plausible.

But this was Edward North who was speaking, a microsurgeon who was known for being slightly eccentric and a bit of a loner. He was awkward enough in social settings for it to be quite surprising to see him attend an event like this at all.

'Yeah, yeah...' Rafael's tone was mocking but he smiled to take any sting from the tone.

As if sensing a sudden tension in the air, Gwen moved away to talk to someone else and he could feel Abbie's fingers stiff and still in his hand now.

Rafael wasn't sure who released the contact first. Maybe it just didn't feel right to be standing here holding hands while they were talking to Edward. Because he'd been the cause of the trouble their marriage was in now?

Or perhaps Abbie had heard that his relationship with this particular colleague had not been the best recently. He *had* been angry with Edward and they'd barely spoken in the last few months, but he'd been justified, hadn't he?

Nobody could deny that Edward was a genius. Thanks to the endless nights he spent on his own reading and researching, he'd been the one to find the information on the experimental treatment that he thought Ella might be a candidate for.

He just wished that Edward had had some idea of the chaos his suggestion would have on his marriage. Had he even been aware of *his* misery in the last few months? Probably not. He wasn't a father himself. As far as Rafael was aware, he wasn't in a long-term relationship either.

Maybe, in his own way, the backhanded compliment disguised as the faux breaking news was his way of apologising. Edward was certainly aware of some undercurrents because he cleared his throat and ran a finger under his collar, as if it was uncomfortable, as he turned towards Abbie.

'How's Ella?' he enquired. 'I heard that she's back in the Lighthouse but…I haven't heard any details about the treatment.'

'It seems to have worked,' Abbie said quietly. 'For a while there, it didn't look like it would but—'

'Something went wrong?' Edward was frowning. 'Not graft versus host disease?' He shook his head. 'No, that wouldn't happen. It's the patient's own T cells that are being reengineered, isn't it? So that they'll recognise and attach to the CD19 protein that's on the surface of B cells.'

'There's another protein,' Abbie told him. 'I'll have to look up what it is for you but it's the same one that's involved with rheumatoid arthritis. Anyway, the levels got very elevated because of the new T cells and Ella became critically ill. She was in the intensive-care unit for weeks.'

Edward looked like he was making a mental note to investigate the unnamed protein himself. 'What did they use to treat her?'

'The same drugs they use for rheumatoid. With quite dramatic results. Her fever and temperature dropped rapidly and she was taken off the ventilator much sooner than any of us had hoped for.'

The atmosphere became even more strained. Edward looked vaguely appalled, as if how dangerous the treatment had been hadn't occurred to him when he'd suggested it.

'It did work in the end,' Abbie said. 'We wouldn't have even known about it if it hadn't been for you. And we couldn't be more grateful.'

We.

They were both looking at him now. It was Rafael's turn to clear his throat. He tilted his head in acknowledgement of his own gratitude. Of course he was grateful for Ella's state of health but he still had the damage to his marriage undermining his happiness. Was it any wonder it was hard to make amends with Edward?

'Thank you,' he said aloud, finally. 'I'm sorry I haven't said so before.'

The apology seemed to be accepted but a new silence fell now and everybody was clearly trying to think of a way to break it. It was Abbie who turned her head and seemed to be looking for someone.

'They're taking a long time, aren't they?'

'Who?' Edward looked puzzled.

'Leo and Lizzie. I know they went for photographs but that was ages ago. They should be back by now. Look at all the new arrivals. The breakfast must be due to start.'

'Oh…didn't you hear? There was a helicopter waiting for them. Leo whisked Lizzie off to go and visit her parents in Brighton.'

'Good grief… *Really*?'

Edward nodded and then shook his head, looking bemused. 'I'd heard they were too sick to come to the wedding but it does seem a little over the top, doesn't it?'

Abbie's smile was tight. 'He loves her. And what a lovely thought, to let them see their daughter in her beautiful dress.'

It seemed that Abbie was uncomfortable talking about the generous gesture. Defensive even. Did a man have to do something a little outrageous to prove how much he loved his bride?

Had he not done enough?

But the low-key service in the registry office hadn't been intended to be the only acknowledgement of their marriage, had it? Rafael had had all sorts of plans for a second wedding and honeymoon in Italy that would have been far more meaningful than a showy helicopter ride. If only Ella hadn't become sick so quickly...

If only...

Edward was looking around, clearly disinterested in discussing the bride's dress. Someone nodded at him and he moved away, looking somewhat relieved. Mitchell Cooper, the American plastic surgeon, and Declan Underwood, another plastic surgeon, who seemed to be here without dates but enjoying themselves, came past Rafael and Abbie, heading for the bar, and Mitchell winked.

'The game is to pick which of the guests has been a former client of the Hunter Clinic,' he murmured. 'I've spotted at least two.'

'And I've spotted the guests of honour returning,' Abbie said. 'I'm going to see if I can find where our table is.'

There was no chance of being alone with Abbie for quite some time, Rafael realised. Watching her disappear into the throng of guests, he had to wonder if she would even want that.

That moment of connection with Abbie during the wedding ceremony that had led to them holding hands was well and truly gone now. The conversation with Edward had been a sobering reminder of how far they still had to go. He followed Mitchell towards the bar. His American colleague was probably searching for a Scotch instead of champagne and Rafael had a sudden desire for something a bit stronger himself.

The group of men at the bar was drawing the attention of every woman in attendance, including those who'd come with partners. And no wonder. Abbie watched them as they raised what looked like glasses of Scotch to toast each other. The dress suits they were all wearing made most men look more attractive but these were already exceptionally good-looking guys.

And Rafael was the best looking of the bunch, as far as she was concerned. His curly dark hair was a little too long, and his features a little sharper than some, but even from a distance she could feel the pull of his Italian passion, the warmth of the fire she knew ran in his blood.

Perhaps she had been too harsh in her reaction to that ultimatum he'd delivered when he'd been so frustrated at not being listened to. Maybe if she understood more about his heritage and the way his male Italian brain worked, she could learn to sort the wheat from the chaff and they could work through their differences, instead of pushing each other away.

Rafael was trying to understand how *her* brain worked. That had been obvious from his line of questioning during Annabelle's surgery. What could she do to let him know that she was just as willing to make an effort?

Ethan had joined the other men at the bar and

he downed a shot of spirits as though it was some kind of medicine. There were certainly undercurrents here for people other than Rafael and herself.

With a sigh, Abbie slipped into her allocated seat at one of the small tables. The chairs had been cleared from the chequerboard marble floor now and no doubt there would be dancing later. After the food and the speeches. Watching Ethan accept another drink from the bar staff, she had to hope that it wouldn't affect his ability to give the speech he was expected to make as best man.

There were choices to be made about the food as the courses came round, which Abbie found very difficult. Not because everything didn't sound absolutely delicious but her appetite seemed to have deserted her. She had to make an effort, though.

'I think I'll have the roast Portland scallops with the fresh pea velouté,' she decided. 'Whatever a velouté is.'

'I believe it's a French word.' Edward was

sharing the table that had been allocated to the de Lucas. 'It means velvet. It's a sauce. Usually a white sauce, but I expect this one might be green.'

Abbie's lips twitched as she caught the twinkle in Edward's otherwise deadpan expression. There was more to this man than people appreciated, wasn't there?

'I'm going to have the Cornish lobster with hand-cut chips,' Rafael decided, when it came to the main course. 'Or perhaps the Aberdeen Angus filet steak with beetroot.'

Except he didn't seem to have any more of an appetite than Abbie did. There was just as much left on his plate as hers when it came time to be cleared away.

The dessert that Abbie chose was to die for. A chocolate fondant with a delectably oozy centre that came with a peach compote and a mascarpone sorbet. The speeches started before she'd taken more than a taste, however, and Abbie stopped and held her breath.

What would Ethan say?

He didn't seem to be showing any effect from the shots of Scotch he'd been throwing back, but then, his speech was so short it was hard to tell. He said something very complimentary about Lizzie and he wished the couple every happiness and that was it. Except that he finished by thanking his brother, saying that he appreciated the way Leo had always looked out for him.

As dessert plates were cleared away, Leo and Lizzie moved through the tables, stopping to talk to as many people as they could before they started the next part of the evening with their first dance. It was Leo who came to the table where Rafael and Abbie were now sitting alone. Edward had gone to talk to Declan.

'Thanks for coming.' Leo smiled. 'I hope you're all enjoying yourselves.'

'It's a beautiful wedding,' Abbie said. 'Lizzie looks stunning.'

'Great speeches, too.' Rafael grinned. 'Short.

If we were in Italy they'd go on till midnight and nobody would get a chance to dance.'

Abbie hoped the length of the best man's speech hadn't been due to the lingering tension between the brothers. 'It was a nice thing that he said,' she offered. 'About you always looking out for him. You must have been an awesome big brother to have.'

Leo's smile looked wry. 'Whether he wanted it or not,' he murmured. 'It wasn't always appreciated.'

Abbie raised her eyebrows but Leo didn't get a chance to answer the silent query. A dramatically glamorous woman, dripping in diamonds, was sailing towards him as gracefully as only an aging prima ballerina could.

'Leo...*darling*... You must come with me. Tony and I are dying to talk to you.' With her arm firmly linked with his, Leo was hustled away.

Abbie had to smile. There would be no prizes for picking her as one of the clinic clients who'd scored an invitation. Everybody knew about Francesca, who had to be in her early seventies now, and had had her first plastic surgeries with Leo and Ethan's father, James.

And that thought led her back to Leo's cryptic comment. She turned to Rafael.

'Whether he wanted it or not? And it wasn't always appreciated? I wonder what that was about?'

Rafael shrugged. 'I've heard the father was a complete bastard. I suspect being the big brother made life pretty tough for Leo.'

'He looks happy now.'

'He just got married to a beautiful woman. Of course he's happy.'

'Where's Ethan?'

'I saw him heading for the restroom a while back.'

'So did I.' Abbie frowned. 'Was it my imagination or was he limping more than usual?'

Rafael mirrored her frown. 'Maybe I should go and check that he's all right.'

'I'll come with you.'

They slipped out of the crowd unnoticed because the music had started and Leo was leading Lizzie onto the dance floor.

They found Ethan in a hallway near the restrooms. Leaning against the wall, with his eyes closed, he didn't see them approach.

'Are you okay?' It was Abbie who asked.

Ethan's eyes snapped open. 'I'm fine,' he said.

He didn't look fine. There were deep lines around his eyes and his skin looked slightly grey. He looked like a man who was dealing with something physically painful.

'Great speech,' Rafael said. 'Well done.'

Ethan gave a noncommittal grunt. 'I didn't say much.'

'Sometimes it doesn't need much,' Abbie said. 'It just needs the right words.'

That brought the ghost of a smile to Ethan's face. 'What are you two doing out here, anyway?' he asked. 'You should be in there, having a good time.' His smile twisted a little. 'Or at

least finding the right words.' He pushed himself off the wall and headed back towards the
ballroom. 'I'm going to find another Scotch.'

Abbie and Rafael looked at each other.

'Shall we go back?' Rafael asked. 'Would you
like to dance?'

Abbie shook her head. 'I think I might have
had enough of so many glamorous people. And
I've certainly had enough champagne.'

Rafael's face emptied of expression. Was he
waiting for her to say that she needed to get back
to the hospital? To Ella?

'You know what I'd really like to do right
now?'

'No. What?'

Abbie reached out and took his hand. Her
heart skipped a beat. This was how she could
show Rafael how much she wanted to try and
fix things.

'I'd like to go home,' she whispered. 'With you.'

CHAPTER EIGHT

STEPPING THROUGH THE door of the apartment in Gloucester Avenue was a bit like sitting with Rafael and waiting for Leo and Lizzie's wedding to begin.

Stepping back in time.

They'd been so excited when they'd found this place. It was perfect. A period conversion that had retained all the character of its origins but had been modernised enough to make it a joy to live in. Tall windows let in lots of light and the polished floorboards made it feel warm and homely. The kitchen and bathrooms had everything they could have wished for. There was central heating and the private garden was walled in and safe for young children. The location was ideal, pretty much halfway between the two places they both worked in—the Hunter Clinic and the Lighthouse Children's Hospital. Best of all, they had Regent's Park and all it had to offer within a few minutes' walk.

It was no surprise that their offer on the apartment was accepted because it was meant to be. So much in love, life just couldn't get any better. The stars were aligned and their perfect future together was just getting started.

So very, very different to the way things were now.

The furniture was all the same, right down to that controversial couch with its big blue throw, but the atmosphere was weird. Empty feeling. There was no excitement about the future lurking in any corners. This felt…awkward.

'There's wine in the fridge.' Rafael was turning on the gas fire to add to the background warmth of the central heating. Did he, too, feel the odd chill of the joy that had gone from these rooms? 'Can I get you a drink?'

'No.' Abbie took off her coat and draped it

over one arm of the couch, dropping her hand-bag beside it. 'I had more than enough champagne at the reception. But you get something if you want to.'

'Maybe later.' Rafael stood with his back to the fire. The intensity of his gaze was unsettling.

It had been Abbie's suggestion to come home with him but now that they were here together for the first time in so many months she wasn't sure that it had been the best idea. What was she going to do now? Throw herself into his arms?

No. That would feel as unnatural as standing here feeling like a stranger in her own home.

Rafael was still staring at her. 'Would you rather go back to the hospital? Are you worried about Ella?'

'No.' Abbie shook her head quickly. 'I know she'll be fine. She won't even wake up until morning. And they'd ring me, anyway, if there was a problem. Oh...' She reached for the hand-bag she'd discarded. 'I forgot that I'd turned my phone off for the wedding ceremony. I'd better switch it back on.'

'I haven't had a call,' Rafael said. 'I had my phone on silent. I never switch it off completely, just in case there's an emergency with a patient. If they hadn't been able to reach you, I'm sure they would have contacted me.'

'Of course.' But Abbie turned her phone on anyway and watched the spinning circle on the screen as it booted up. She put it down as she realised that her diverted attention was only making it feel more awkward for Rafael but almost as soon as the device was out of her hands it sounded a message alert.

Her gaze snagged on Rafael's and held there for a heartbeat. And then he turned away with a flash of something like defeat washing over his face.

She had given him hope, hadn't she, saying that she wanted to go home with him? Now it seemed like Ella was about to come between them again.

'It's probably just Melanie telling me that everything's fine.'

But she had to look.

And it wasn't about Ella at all.

Another heartbeat and all Abbie could do was close her eyes tightly as she clutched the phone against her chest with both hands.

Dio…

What the hell had been in that message?

Something devastating, by the look of her. Rafael was in front of Abbie in only a couple of steps. He gripped her arms.

'*Che cosa*? What has happened?'

Abbie struggled to take an inward breath. 'It's not about Ella,' she whispered.

'Then what? What has made you look like this? *Tell* me…'

'It's…it's…Toby.'

Rafael felt his heart stop for a split second and then thump painfully back into action. Who the hell was Toby? Had Abbie met someone else?'

'Toby?' His voice felt raw. 'He's someone in New York?'

Abbie nodded mutely. Her eyes were still tightly shut and she was clearly on the verge of tears.

Maybe it didn't matter who this Toby was. What mattered was that he could feel Abbie shaking under his hands. She needed support. Comfort.

Love…

He pulled Abbie right into the circle of his arms and held her against his heart. He didn't say anything because he had no idea what he *could* say. And he didn't need to say anything anyway because moments later words began to spill out of Abbie between wrenching sobs.

'He was only five…and he was such a brave little boy… He was getting the same treatment as Ella and his mum and I became good friends. Shelley was crying when we left…she said she'd miss us both so much but…but knowing that Ella had made it through was giving her strength…

the suffering that poor little Toby was going through would all be worth it in the end because…because one day soon she'd be able to take him home to his daddy…the way…the way I was taking Ella home…to *you*…'

The words got strangled by the heartbroken sobs for some time after that. Rafael simply held Abbie and rocked her gently until the grief subsided. Clearly this little boy hadn't survived the treatment.

It could so easily have been Ella.

Rafael's throat tightened and he could feel an odd prickling sensation at the back of his eyes. *Tears*?

No. Not possible. He hadn't cried since he'd been a very small boy. A man's pride didn't allow the showing of such weakness. He needed a distraction but there was none to be had at this moment. No work to be done. He couldn't even pick up a journal article and lose himself in that for a while. And then Abbie made it even worse.

'It could have been Ella,' she choked out, echoing his own terrible thought. 'I could have put her through all that suffering for nothing. Shelley must be feeling so *awful.*'

'She'll know that she tried everything she could to keep her little one alive. That it was the right thing to do.'

But Abbie was shaking her head as she tried to pull away from him. Rafael loosened his hold but still kept her within the circle of his arms.

'I just didn't think. I couldn't see your point of view at all. Ella could have died, just like Toby, and all that suffering would have been pointless and…and, worse…we would have been half a world away from you. You would never have been able to hold Ella again. It was wrong, Rafael…' Tears were streaming down Abbie's face. 'I'm *sorry.*'

Strangely, any threat of his own tears had evaporated. Rafael felt strong. He brushed tears from Abbie's face.

'*Si*, it could have been Ella but it *wasn't* so I

was wrong, too. We were both wrong. Isn't it time that we forgave each other?'

Abbie was nodding. Her sob became a hiccup and, instead of pushing out against the circle of his arms, she moved closer, lifting her own arms to wrap them around his neck.

This embrace wasn't about offering comfort or support. This was a new closeness. An affirmation of forgiveness.

It was Rafael who pulled back this time. So that he could cup Abbie's face with his hands as he kissed her forehead and then her closed eyelids. Slowly. Softly.

He felt her eyes open as he finished the third kiss. And then they were looking at each other, the way they had when Leo and Lizzie had been kissing at the end of their wedding ceremony and it had seemed the most natural thing in the world to kiss his own wife at that point.

Just like it did now.

Oh...*God*...

This was what she had been aching for. The

tenderness of those gentle kisses in the wake of an emotional storm that had washed away anything irrelevant.

Was this what forgiveness felt like?

If so, it was incredibly sweet.

Healing.

And then Abbie became aware of more than the calm after the storm. She could feel the softness of Rafael's lips as they pressed so gently on her eyelids. She could feel the strength in his hands as he cradled her face. She had to open her eyes then and when she did, all she could see in his eyes was the caring.

The *love*.

She could feel herself rising to stand on tiptoe. To meet his lips with her own. They were so close right now. Closer than they'd been for a long time. Maybe closer than they'd ever been emotionally.

But it wasn't close enough.

Abbie wanted more. She wanted them to be skin to skin. To have Rafael touching her in a way that would affirm life, rather than provide comfort in the face of death.

'Take me to bed, Rafe,' she whispered. 'Please.'

Without a word, Rafael scooped her up into his arms and strode through the apartment without pausing to turn on any more lights. Their bedroom had French doors that opened into the private garden and there were lights beyond that. Enough to take the edge off the darkness in the room. And Abbie didn't need more than that. Her other senses were more than enough.

She could hear the slide of fabric as Rafael peeled off his shirt, the thump of shoes being heeled off and the scratch of the zip as he got rid of his trousers. She could feel her own fingers shaking as she tried to undo the fastenings of her dress and she could hear the catch of her breath that was almost a gasp as Rafael's hands closed over hers and took over the task.

It was colder in here, away from the fire. Rafael pulled the duvet from the bed and draped it over Abbie's shoulders as she sat there while he took off her shoes and tights. And then he somehow wrapped them both in the fluffy, light down of the cover and they were lying on the bed with Rafael half over her and he was holding her face again as he kissed her.

A kiss that started as gently as the one during the wedding service. There was almost wonder in it. He was treating her as something fragile and precious. But Abbie was kissing him back now. She knew the first slide of her tongue against his would ignite the same kind of passion that had been unleashed with that kiss in the changing room and that was what she needed. She pushed closer with her hips, too, to feel more of his body as she opened her mouth to him and deepened the kiss.

A rough sound came from deep within Rafael's chest and his hands were moving now. Swiftly tracing the outline of her body. Pausing to shape her breasts and bring her nipples to painful hardness, and then they were moving lower. Sliding over her hips and touching her exactly where it ached most.

It was Abbie's turn to cry out incoherently. She didn't want slow and tender. Not this time. She pushed against his hand and used her hand to reach for the hardness she knew she would find without breaking the rhythm as their tongues danced and passion spiralled to bright flames.

Rafael changed his position with the smoothness that could only come from the confidence of knowing someone so intimately. Her body welcomed him as if it had only been yesterday they had last made love and they were in total accord about the pace of this fiercely passionate coupling. They both knew it would be over too soon. But they also both knew that it would be very different next time. This was a release of tension that had become pent up enough to be destructive all by itself. And it was a statement, too. An underscoring of the forgiveness perhaps.

Whatever emotional currents ran beneath the physical communication, the hard, fast sex left a curiously calm aftermath. It took some time for their heart rates to drop and for both of them to catch their breath enough to be able to talk. Abbie was content to lie there in Rafael's arms, their heads on the same pillow and their noses almost touching.

'I've missed you so much,' she whispered. 'I've missed *this*.'

Rafael only had to tilt his face up a little to kiss the tip of her nose. And then her lips. The sound he made was one of absolute agreement.

'*Ti voglio molto bene,*' he murmured. '*Sei tutto per me. E...e ho bisogno di te.*'

A smile curled the corners of Abbie's mouth. She'd learned more Italian than she'd realised in her time with Rafael.

'I love you very much, too,' she said softly. 'You are everything to me as well. And...and I do need you, too. Very much.' But then she caught her bottom lip between her teeth. 'Is it enough, do you think? That we love each other?'

'*Si.*' The word was adamant. 'Of course it is.'

For a while they lay there in silence. Abbie hoped Rafael was right but they'd always loved each other like this, hadn't they? And it hadn't been enough when it had come to the crunch over Ella's treatment.

It was Rafael who broke the silence. 'You understand Italian very well now, *cara*. It's time I took you to see my birthplace. To meet my family. I've kept them shut away from this for too long already.'

'They'd been about to come, hadn't they? Your mother and your sister? Just after Ella was born.'

'And then she got sick and was in isolation and I told them nobody could come. I couldn't tell anybody about the…difficulties we were having after you'd gone to New York but my mother still called every week or two. She wants to know why she can't meet her *nipote*. Why I'm not allowing her to meet my bride. "What's so wrong with us?" she asks. "What's wrong with her?"'

'Oh, help…' Being estranged from her own parents had made Abbie focus on nothing more than the nuclear family she and Rafael had made with Ella. How selfish had she been, not realising the ripple effect this had all had on Rafael's relationship with his own family? He was Italian. Family was everything. 'I'm going to be very nervous about meeting my in-laws now.'

'It will be fine. They will all love you. And they will adore Fiorella. It will only get harder if we leave it too long so we should do this as soon as our little Fiorella is well enough to travel.'

'I'd love that. I've heard so much about how beautiful the Almafi Coast is.'

'It's beyond beauty. The ancient villages that cling to the rocky cliffs. The sparkling blue of the sea. The scent of lemon trees and sunshine...'

Abbie blinked. 'You sound...homesick, Rafe.'

She could feel his whole body move with the shrug that was automatic. 'Perhaps I am, a little. Not so much for the place but for the memories of childhood. The...the safety?'

Abbie understood. 'It was so much easier, wasn't it? Having other people make the big decisions. Knowing that, whatever happened, there would always be a place to call home. People to love you.'

'This is home now.' Rafael kissed her again. *'Our* home.'

'It won't really be home, though, will it? Until Ella is here.'

'Family,' Rafael agreed on a sigh. *'Si...'*

'I'm glad you had a happy childhood, Rafe. That's all I want for Ella.'

'I had brother and sisters. And cousins. Lots of family. She will be welcomed with open hearts.'

And maybe she would have some brothers or sisters of her own one day. But that was a dream Abbie wasn't ready to share aloud. This new space they were in felt too fragile to test the boundaries.

'Your parents are still together, aren't they?'

'*Si*. They probably still argue with each other all the time and complain that neither of them listens to the other but they will always be together, I think. For the sake of the family.'

'I don't want to be like that,' Abbie said. 'I don't want to be together just for Ella. Or to keep up an illusion of family. And…and I don't want us to argue all the time.'

'We will be together because we truly love each other.' She could see Rafael's smile. 'But…I am Italian…I can't promise there will never be a disagreement.'

'As long as we talk.' The words were urgent. 'And *listen* to each other. And try to understand.'

'We will. I promise you that.'

Would even that be enough? 'I look at my parents,' Abbie whispered. 'And the way things fell apart after Sophie died. The way they backed out of our lives as soon as they knew Ella was sick. Was it because they didn't love each other enough that it destroyed them? That they didn't love *me* enough?' Her words wobbled this time.

'*I* love you enough,' Rafael said fiercely. 'You have to believe that.'

His hands were moving over her body again

now. Slowly, this time, as he stopped any further conversation by covering her lips with his.

And once again they were in total accord. They didn't need fierce, hot sex now. They needed the comfort of slow, tender lovemaking. An affirmation of love rather than life. Healing for things that went a long way further back than the troubles in their own relationship.

This certainly wasn't about pushing issues out of sight by distracting themselves with physical passion.

This was new. Making love with the depth of a new understanding about each other. A new resolution to make things work.

A whole new dimension to the love they shared.

A long time later, for the first time ever, Abbie found slow tears trickling down her face in the aftermath of lovemaking.

Rafael was horrified. 'You're crying, *cara*.'

'It's okay,' she whispered. 'They're happy tears.'

'Like at a wedding?'

'*Si...*' Abbie's smile wobbled. 'Exactly like at a wedding.'

Happy tears.

That was all right, then.

Rafael could hear Abbie's breathing slowing a little. Feel her relax even more in his arms as she drifted into sleep. He would not sleep yet. Not until he was sure that she didn't need anything more from him in the way of comfort. Or love.

Everything was all right again. This was exactly what they had needed. Where they needed to be.

In their own home.

Their own bed. Where he could show Abbie how much he loved her. Apologies had been made and accepted. They had forgiven each other.

They had both been wrong but they had put it behind them. Admitting fault meant that honour could be restored. Forgiveness meant that pride could be smoothed.

Si...

They could move forward again now. All of them, including his little Fiorella.

Mia famiglia.

It was with a smile on his lips that Rafael finally allowed himself to sink into slumber.

CHAPTER NINE

'IT'S LOOKING GOOD.'

'Yes. The retainers have done a good job bringing the tissues closer together.'

'The parents need a lot of the credit. It can't be easy keeping those retainers in place when you've got a baby that needs feeding and washing.'

'And when he's miserable and doing his best to pull things off his face.'

'I guess you do what you have to do when it's your baby.'

'Mmm.'

A quick shared glance spoke volumes between the two surgeons. The theatre staff around them also exchanged similar glances. Who knew better than the de Lucas how hard it could be, doing what you had to do for your baby?

Baby Angus MacDonald looked tiny, lying on the operating table. His eyes were being held closed by wide pieces of tape. His mouth was held open by retractors that hooked over the top and bottom lips. A breathing tube was as far out of the way as it could be to one side. Rafael was putting the final stitches into closing both the baby's hard and soft palates.

Now it was Abbie's turn. She studied the tiny face, using callipers to measure the space between the nostrils and the lips. There were two clefts to repair here and she had to mark the skin carefully so that her final rows of neat stitching would make straight lines from the centre of the nostrils to the lips. She created a map of tiny dots of indelible ink.

'Local?'

'Please.' The less bleeding that occurred as she used the scalpel the better as far as making the cuts as accurate as possible.

The incisions were a Z shape. Excess muscle and fat was removed so that the surface tissue would fit together with absolute precision. Rafael was ready with the cautery to seal blood vessels. A theatre nurse held a pair of scissors to snip off the ends of the stitches as Abbie deftly looped and tied the thin suture material.

It was so satisfying to pull the tissue together and see it nestle into exactly the position that she had mapped out. Nobody would see the precise work Rafael had achieved inside Angus's mouth and Abbie hoped that, eventually, nobody would see what she had done here, on the outside. In a few years' time, these scars should be invisible.

It wasn't the end of this surgery, however. The baby's nostrils were an odd, flattened shape due to the birth deformity and that was something else they could fix in this operation. Not only could they pull the tissue inside the nostrils together to make them a normal shape, they could ensure that the passages inside were clear enough to improve breathing. She and Rafael worked together on this last task and thirty minutes later they stood back as a nurse gently wiped the little face clean.

'His parents are going to be thrilled when they see how he looks,' she said.

There was a murmur of agreement around the table. Apart from the two lines of visible stitching and the lips being more swollen than they should be, this was a normal-looking baby. A beautiful little boy.

This time, when Abbie looked up to the space between Rafael's mask and theatre cap she could see the crinkles at the corners of his eyes and she knew he was smiling.

'Good job, Mrs de Luca.'

'Likewise, Mr de Luca.'

Another murmur of general agreement was accompanied by a ripple of laughter this time. The atmosphere was relaxed and happy. Not only was this surgery a great success but the de Lucas were obviously working well together again.

The "dream team" was back in action.

And it wasn't just in Theatre that they were

working well together again. After watching that Angus had no problem coming out from under the anaesthetic, Abbie hurried to catch up with Rafael in the changing room.

'I've got them,' she said.

'Got what, *cara*?'

'The colour charts. Melanie's boyfriend works in a paint shop and she says that if we choose the colour, they can deliver it for us any time. They can do all the brushes and rollers and everything, too.' She opened the door of her locker and shifted the clothes and shoes she had left in there. A moment later she held up some glossy brochures triumphantly.

'Are you sure you want to do this? We've never done any decorating ourselves. We might be better to get some experts to come and do it for us.'

'That would take ages. Mel says that good firms are booked up months in advance. And it's easy…'

Rafael didn't look convinced.

'Ella's due for her biopsy in a few days. If it's good news then we're going to be allowed to take her home soon. Don't you want us to have her room all ready for her?'

They were both assuming that the news would be good. How could it not be when Ella was looking so well? The time that Abbie and Rafael had spent with their daughter over the last few days since the wedding had been a joy.

The time they had found to be together at home had also been a joy. They had started talking properly about the immediate future. About wanting to get the garden sorted so that Ella could play out there and use her swing in the summer. About turning the room they'd never had the chance to really use as a nursery into a bedroom fit for a princess.

'You really want to do this, don't you?'

Abbie nodded. It wasn't just to have a pretty new room ready for their daughter. This was something they could do together. Another way to build on the foundations they were laying for their future together.

'I've already found a colour that would be perfect. Look…'

'*Dio.*' Rafael eyed the square Abbie was pointing to. 'It's very…pink, isn't it?'

'It's exactly the same shade as that ballerina bear you gave her. There's a catalogue here of friezes you can get and there's one with pink teddies on it.' Abbie shuffled through the handful of pamphlets she held. 'And I thought we could do silver stars on the ceiling. You get a template and you can spray paint them on and put glitter on while the paint's still wet.'

Rafael closed his eyes for a moment.

'We can do this, Rafe. Maybe it won't be perfect but does that really matter?'

She watched him take a deep breath. 'When do you want to start?'

'Tonight. After Ella's settled. We could get some take-aways from our favourite Italian restaurant to have after we've done some painting.'

* * *

By eleven that night, there was a deep-dish lasagne still in the oven that had probably dried out to the point of being inedible. Abbie had streaks of pink paint on her nose and in her hair and the one wall they had finished painting looked terrible, with splotches of its original colour showing through all over the place.

'It just needs another coat,' Abbie said. But she looked close to tears.

Rafael wanted to say that he knew it would have been a better idea to get the experts in but he bit his tongue and kept scrubbing at the drips of paint on the polished wooden floor.

In the silence that followed he glanced up to see Abbie just standing, looking dejectedly at the wall. A roller dangled from one hand. Her shoulders were slumped. The pink stripe in her hair had come from pushing stray strands back towards her ponytail. The ancient T-shirt of his that she was wearing to cover her clothes might not be something she would ever wear in public but her stance reminded him of when he'd seen her again after her long absence.

When she'd been standing outside Ella's room and he'd realised how hard it had all been for her. He'd wanted to put his arms around her then and tell her how much he loved her. That everything would be all right. That he would never let life be this hard for her again.

He hadn't been able to bridge the gulf between them then.

But he could now.

What did it matter if there were pink marks left on these floorboards? Rafael got to his feet. He stood behind Abbie and wrapped his arms around her, loving the way she leaned back into him without hesitation.

'Paint always looks bad before it dries,' he said with conviction.

'How do you know that? Have you ever painted a wall before?'

'I just know,' Rafael said. 'And if it doesn't look good when it dries, then we'll just give it another coat. And another and another until it looks perfect.'

Abbie groaned. 'Why do rooms need to have *four* walls?'

Rafael laughed. 'We need to eat. And then we need to shower.' He held up the cloth he was still holding in one hand. 'I can get all that pink paint off your skin. I have been practising.'

'I'm too tired to eat. Couldn't we just go to bed?'

Tempting. But it would have to wait. Rafael shook his head. 'Food,' he said.

'Is that an order?' Abbie was smiling as she swivelled in his arms to look up at him but then her smile faltered. What had been intended as a joke had an undercurrent that had the potential to reopen old wounds. Her mouth twisted into a grimace. 'I'm too tired to think,' she sighed. 'I *hope* it's an order.' Her smile reappeared. 'Feed me. Please?'

The following evening Rafael made sure they ate before they started work on Ella's room. Thai food tonight, instead of Italian. Maybe they could do Turkish or good old English fish and chips next time.

There were parts of this project that were very enjoyable. Cleaning up afterwards, for example. Long, hot showers where they could soap each other's skin and linger in one spot.

'Pink paint,' he'd say. How Abbie might have got so much pink paint on her breasts was open to debate but she didn't seem to mind his ministrations.

He certainly hadn't dripped any pink paint inside his trousers but he wasn't going to complain about Abbie's attention to certain parts of *his* anatomy either.

It even worked when they were out of the shower. When he wanted to take his time to taste her skin.

'Must have missed a bit,' he would murmur as he licked. 'Pink paint.'

It made Abbie giggle and the code slipped into that special place that was the private language of people who loved each other. A way of saying so much with only a look or a word or two that would make no sense to anybody else.

Eating together was another very enjoyable part of these snatched hours together. Not just because they could share the food and the feeling of home but because it meant they could talk about their days the way they'd done when they'd first known each other.

'It's a giant mole.' Abbie had a new patient to tell him about on the night they finally finished the last coat of pink paint. 'Covering her whole lower leg. I'm going to insert saline pouches under the skin of her good leg and we'll inflate them gradually over the next few months until we get enough new skin.'

'And then you'll remove the mole?'

'Yes. And we'll keep the skin attached to its source until it's established a blood supply and got locked into its new location. Means we'll have to keep the legs splinted together for quite a while but it'll be worth it. Her mother's happy to do it.'

Rafael had news to share on the night they glued the teddy-bear frieze into position half-way up the walls.

'Anoosheh met her adoptive parents today. She's going to have brothers and sisters and they've got a pet rabbit. She's very excited.'

'That's fantastic. You must be so happy about that.'

'I am.' It had, in fact, been surprising how happy the news had made him feel. Even more so than the excellent result that was appearing from the first major surgery the little girl had needed.

Maybe he was changing. Learning to see things more like Abbie?

'Ooh...' Abbie paused in her task of trying to get the air bubbles out from beneath the strip of frieze. 'Do you think Ella would like a pet rabbit?'

'She has Ears. I don't think we need to rush into getting a real one.'

'No…I guess not. I just thought it might be a nice birthday present.'

'She's had her birthday.'

'Yes, but we were in New York. And she was too sick to celebrate. I thought…maybe we could have another birthday party? When she gets home?'

'Coming home will be enough to celebrate all by itself, won't it?'

Abbie was standing very still now. Her eyes were huge. She opened her mouth to say something but nothing came out so she nodded instead.

Rafael couldn't find anything to say to fill the silence either. Perhaps it was because Ella was due to have her bone-marrow biopsy tomorrow. He stepped forward to take the sponge out of Abbie's hand. What did it matter if there were air bubbles under the frieze for ever? It was time they stopped working and went to bed. Time they held each other for a while and gathered strength for what would undoubtedly be a tense day.

This was the first major procedure that Rafael had seen Ella undergo since before they'd left for New York.

How would he handle it?

Would he even want to be present?

Apparently he wanted to be more than simply present. It was Rafael who held Ella in Theatre as the powerful sedative took hold and Abbie could sense his tension skyrocket as their baby lost consciousness.

Rafael was curled protectively over their daughter as her head lolled sideways, using the crook of his elbow to support her neck and his hand to catch the tiny arm that flopped like a rag doll's.

Abbie could remember the first time she'd held Ella under the same circumstances and that terrible moment when she'd gone so boneless and still in her arms. The awful thought that she couldn't hold back.

This is what it will feel like when she dies...

Was that what Rafael was thinking as he laid Ella down on the bed so gently? Abbie's throat tightened painfully. A nurse made sure that the little head was positioned well on the special pillow and the young registrar assisting the oncology consultant tilted Ella's head back to ensure that her airway was protected.

Rafael came to stand beside Abbie as they prepared Ella for aspirating the sample of her bone marrow that would tell them what was happening on a cellular level. A lab technician was arranging a series of slides on the top of a trolley that she would prepare as soon as the sample had been obtained. Another trolley was covered with the bone-marrow aspiration kit, which included intimidating items like long needles with handle-type attachments, along with the usual plastic syringes, needles and a scalpel.

Ella was moved carefully into a recovery-type

position, with her knees flexed, and then the skin over the back of her hip was swabbed with disinfectant and covered with a sterile drape that had a small square window in it.

'So, it's the posterior iliac crest that's being used.' Rafael's voice sounded tight. 'The last time I saw this, it was the tibia that was used.'

Was he trying to distance himself from what was going on by looking at it in a professional sense? Was it the only form of protection he thought he had?

'It's been the iliac crest for the last few times,' Abbie responded. 'The tibia's only a suitable site for very young babies. It's too hard to get the sample and there's the risk of causing a fracture.' Her voice was just as tight. She *hated* watching this.

Her tone must have carried because the consultant looked up from where she was infiltrating the area around Ella's hip with local anaesthetic.

'You don't have to stay,' she said, with a sympathetic smile. 'You could go for a walk maybe.

Or get a coffee. We'll come and get you as soon as it's all over. Ella's sound asleep. She doesn't know if you're here or not.'

'*We* know.' The words were ground out of Rafael as if uttering them was painful.

There was no professional distance in insisting that they stay in the room. Abbie knew that there was nowhere for Rafael to hide in that moment. That he was vulnerable. She also knew that there was another way to protect yourself. One that she had yearned for so often when she'd been in New York.

Could she get over the resentment of not having it and offer it to Rafael right now?

Of course she could. She *loved* him, didn't she?

Abbie reached for his hand and squeezed it, offering some of her own strength. An acknowledgment that she understood exactly how he was feeling. That they were in this together.

She offered an encouraging smile, too, as her hand was squeezed back, hard enough to crush her fingers painfully. She was sure the results of this test were going to be good. That putting Ella through this procedure was worthwhile.

Impossible not to feel a little sick, though, watching that big needle around the stylet being twisted into their baby's hip bone. The top of the needle was unscrewed and the stylet removed and then a syringe was attached. You could almost feel the pain that the suction that was needed to try and aspirate the bone marrow would have caused if the patient had been conscious. That first attempt wasn't successful, so the stylet had to go back in and the needle advanced a little further.

And all the time Abbie could feel how tense Rafael was. Closing her eyes, she got a real sense of the struggle he must have gone through when Ella had been so tiny. How gut-wrenching it had been for him to see his baby undergoing this kind of procedure when the professional side of his brain must have been not only trying to protect him but arming him with the statistics of how remote the possibility of a cure was.

Whereas Abbie had focussed only on any tiny gleam of hope. When the only protection she'd had had been the comfort of Rafael's arms. Had she given as much comfort as she'd received?

Probably not. Rafael had taken on board the suffering of the woman he loved as well as their baby's suffering.

No wonder he'd reached breaking point. When it had all become too much.

Abbie tightened her grip on Rafael's hand. As gruelling as this was, she had never felt closer to him. She could only hope that he was feeling the same.

Rafael had to consciously control the pressure he was putting into holding Abbie's hand because he knew that if he squeezed as hard as he wanted to he would cause her physical pain.

And causing pain to someone he loved was

simply abhorrent to him, whether that pain was physical or emotional.

He loved Abbie with all his heart and he'd never wanted to cause her pain by not being there to support her when she was watching things like this. But his love for Ella was different. She was an actual *part* of his heart. Of his soul. He could feel her pain as keenly as if this procedure and the countless others that had come before this one were being performed on him.

And how could anyone justify continuing to inflict pain like that when the likelihood of success was so remote?

The weight of that pain and the darkness hovering in the future had been all that Rafael had been able to see.

But Abbie had been able to see the glimmer of hope and, this time, Rafael could see it too. If these results were good, Ella's central line would be taken out tomorrow. They would be able to take her home very, very soon.

He turned his head and, as if sensing the subtle movement, Abbie looked up and caught his gaze.

The love he could see in her eyes made his throat tighten so much he couldn't take a new breath but he could feel his lips curl in a gentle smile as his gaze clung to hers.

I love you, too, was the silent message. *I think I understand now.*

The second attempt at aspiration was successful. The lab technician was dotting what looked like dark blood onto the slides and then using another slide to smear the sample over the glass. They would be ready for staining and microscopic examination of the cells in no time at all. The registrar was holding test tubes with additional small amounts of the bone marrow, tipping them end to end to mix the anticoagulant and make sure that these samples didn't clot and become useless.

They would have the results very quickly.

And it was all over. The needle was out and the nurse had a dressing she was using to apply pressure to the almost invisible wound. The registrar was drawing up the medication to reverse the sedation.

Ella was a little grizzly as she began waking up properly.

'You carry her back to the ward,' Abbie said to Rafael. 'She's probably hungry more than anything after being nil by mouth this morning. I'll bet she lets you give her a bottle when we get her settled back in her room.'

Rafael was more than happy to oblige. He carried Ella in his arms, jiggling her gently to try and comfort her. Even being back in her room with Ears and ballerina bear didn't seem to distract her and she made it very clear she wasn't interested in having a bottle, from either her father or her mother.

She was still unhappy half an hour later.

'Is she in pain, do you think?'

Abbie shook her head. 'They put lots more local in when they finish the procedure and she's got paracetamol on board. I've never seen her react like this after an aspiration before. Try her with the bottle again.'

'You try first this time.'

But Ella wouldn't drink her milk, even with Abbie holding the bottle and cuddling her in the chair. She pushed it away with her little fists and cried harder.

Rafael tried reading her a story and making animal noises but it couldn't provide a distraction and it only made him feel foolish so he gave up. Abbie tried singing songs but petered out just as quickly. Even her beloved toy Ears was roundly rejected time and again and he ended up abandoned on the floor.

Ella was exhausted but still whimpering when the oncology consultant came to visit.

'The news couldn't be better,' the consultant told them. 'There's no evidence of the cancer whatsoever and the new T cells are still there, ready to fight any recurrence.'

Abbie burst into tears at the news. Rafael had

to swallow very hard before he could produce any words.

'Thank you,' was all he could manage. 'Thank you *so* much.'

But the consultant's smile was fading already. 'She's not sounding too happy, is she?'

'She's been like this ever since the aspiration,' Abbie said. 'I don't understand. She's never re-acted like this before.'

'She's breathing fast.' The consultant stepped closer to where Abbie was holding Ella, rock-ing her. 'And she's feeling rather warm, don't you think?'

'She's been crying for a long time.'

'She must still be in pain,' Rafael said. 'Can we not give her something more for it?'

'I don't think it's her hip that's bothering her.' The consultant was frowning as her fingers pressed against Ella's upper arm, taking her pulse. 'I want a full set of vital signs done and a blood count.' She looked from Abbie to Rafael.

'I don't want to worry you but I have a feeling she might have picked up a bug of some kind.'

The blood-test results came back almost as fast as the results on the bone marrow had, but this time the news was very different.

Thanks to the strain on her immune system for so long, Ella had been unable to fight off whatever infection had sneaked past all their precautions.

Her cancer might have been beaten but there was a new enemy to fight now and it looked like a fierce one.

Over the rest of that day Ella's condition deteriorated bit by bit. Her heart and breathing rate increased. Her oxygen saturation dropped. Her temperature climbed. Various specialists were called in to assess her and, by that evening, they were all looking concerned.

'I'm so sorry,' one of them said to Rafael and Abbie, 'but this is looking serious. I'm afraid we need to shift Ella to Intensive Care.'

CHAPTER TEN

THEY'D BEEN HERE before but this was different.

The end of the road?

Abbie was beyond exhausted.

Beyond hope?

Ella had been intubated shortly after arriving in the intensive-care unit and the breathing tube attached to the ventilator had quickly been joined by other invasive monitoring devices, including an arterial line to measure blood gases, a second venous line to administer fluids, a urinary catheter and a nasogastric tube. She was transferred to an isolation room, X-rays taken and antibiotics started.

Now all they could do was watch and wait. To try and offer life support until such time as Ella's tiny body could muster the resources to overcome whatever new enemy had made its un-welcome appearance. The decisions that might need to be made if the situation got any worse were just too awful to contemplate.

They'd been so close to victory.

So close to fitting all those pieces of the perfect life back together again where they could have made a picture that was stronger and brighter than it had ever been before.

But now the colours had been muted. Virtu-ally erased. Everything looked clinical and white and frightening in here. The only hint of col-our around Ella was the faded pink of the be-draggled old toy, Ears, which Abbie had insisted on bringing with them and which now sagged forlornly at the far end of her bed, well out of the way. The sparkly pink ballerina bear had been left behind in the ward, seemingly along with all the other bright colours and hopes. Even Ella's pretty pink pyjamas were gone. She wore nothing more than a nappy in this warm space because her chest had to be bare due to all the electrodes that were stuck to her skin and easy access was needed to all the tubes invading her small body.

The sparkle of that new closeness with Rafael had gone, too. Things felt brittle between them again. As tense as they had been when she'd returned with Ella from New York. Far too similar to what things had been like just before she'd left when huge decisions had had to be made and they had been on such different pages. Just before that terrible row that had ended the marriage they'd had until then.

They were both in this small space with their daughter but the gap between them had widened. For Abbie it was too close to where she'd been when Ella had been so sick in New York and she had been there by herself, watching every breath her baby had taken in case it had been her last. Feeling…betrayed, because Rafael hadn't been there beside her.

He *was* here physically now but he seemed to be distancing himself, just like he had in the past. Standing back emotionally and weighing up whether it was fair to put a tiny person through so much suffering when...when there was no hope?

He was sitting on a chair in the corner of the room at the moment, his head tipped back and his eyes closed. His face was grey but neither of them had had any sleep since Ella had been brought into this intense place where small lives hovered between life and death. She hoped he was actually asleep now and not just trying to shut himself further away but it seemed unlikely given that two of the PICU doctors and a nurse were in here, quietly reassessing their newest admission after her first twelve hours of intensive care.

There *had* to be hope. Surely Abbie would be able to find it again when the stunning effect of this new blow wore off? Or when a new blood-test result came in that showed that one of the raft of antibiotics and other drugs was already helping to get the infection under control.

Abbie stared at the bank of monitors around the bed as the doctors spoke quietly to each other.

'Have you got a blood-gas syringe there?'

'Yes. Here it is. Do you want venous samples as well?'

'Yes. Let's get a full blood count and electrolytes. We need to keep a close eye on renal function, too.'

'What's the central pressure at the moment?'

'Down to nine. Let's get some more fluids up. I don't want it dropping any further.'

'Happy with sedation levels?'

'Yes. We'll keep the fentanyl and midazolam infusion going.'

The tracing of Ella's heartbeat blipped across the screen. Too fast but at least it was steady. Even a single missed beat right now and it might be too much for Abbie. She stared at the screen, willing it to continue.

One of the doctors handed a tiny syringe of arterial blood to the nurse, who whisked it away

to test the oxygen levels. He checked all the figures being displayed on the ventilator and then
glanced sideways.

'How are you doing, Abbie?'

Abbie shrugged. Goodness…had she caught
such an Italian gesture from Rafael? She tried
to swallow the huge lump in her throat.

'Oh…you know. We…really weren't expecting this…'

'I know.' The tone was full of sympathy. The
doctor turned to look at Rafael. 'Things are stable at the moment. You two look like you need
some rest. You know there's a bed that you can
use? The nurse can show you where it is. You
could take it in turns to get a bit of sleep.'

Rafael's eyes opened slowly, revealing how
aware he was of everything going on in the
room. 'I'm not going anywhere,' he said. 'Not
this time.'

For a short time, when the doctors had done
all they could for the moment, Rafael and Abbie
were left alone with their daughter.

'Are you going to call your parents?'

Abbie shook her head. Any hope of the birth of a grandchild ending the estrangement had evaporated when her parents had disappeared from contact after learning that Ella was so sick. Such an obvious lack of support was the last thing she needed to be reminded of right now.

She only had Rafael, didn't she?

She'd thought he would be all she ever needed in the way of family but the way he was pulling into himself with this latest crisis was leaving her feeling horribly isolated.

Desperately frightened, in fact.

Abbie had believed she was over the grief of losing the closeness she should have had with her own parents but it wasn't buried that deeply, after all, was it?

'Are you going to call yours?'

'*Si*. Of course.' But Rafael rubbed at his forehead and pushed his fingers through his hair. 'Even if it will worry them, they need to know. They are *la mia famiglia*. Fiorella's family.'

It was much later in the day before Rafael took the time to call Italy, however, and when he came back he went straight to Ella's bedside, where he stood staring down at the unconscious baby, resting a hand lightly on the top of her head. He looked tense enough to explode into a million shards.

'What's wrong?' Abbie asked.

'My mother…I can't believe she didn't tell me. She said she didn't want to worry me and it was nothing. But it's *not* nothing… It's…' The hand that wasn't touching Ella curled into a fist.

Abbie's heart sank to a new low. The world was spinning out of control with increasing intensity. 'What's happened?'

'My father. Apparently he had a heart attack two days ago.'

'Oh, my God… How bad was it?'

'I don't know. I need to clear my head a little before I try and ring the hospital. My mother's version of events was somewhat garbled. She said he's fine. That my father was far too stubborn to let something like a heart attack kill him.'

'Is *she* all right?'

A huff of sound came from Rafael. 'She made it sound as if it's nothing more than a head cold. As if…as if she doesn't actually *care*.'

The shaft of pain in Abbie's chest made her wonder if it was physically possible for a little piece of heart to break off.

Rafael was a passionate man who cared very deeply about the people he loved but had he been taught at an early age to step back from the worst of the pain that that sort of caring brought with it? To use *dis*passion as protection?

That would explain so much.

'You know that's not true,' she said softly. 'You know she cares very much. She's trying to protect you. Protect *herself*…'

Rafael stood there motionless for a long moment and then gave a terse nod. 'I'm sure you're right. They might have always fought a lot but they'd be lost without each other. She must be very afraid at the moment.'

'Why don't you go and ring the hospital? Ella's good. There's been no change.'

Good was hardly the word to describe Ella's condition, but while there'd been no improvement neither had there been any further deterioration, and maybe that was enough to qualify as 'good' for now.

It was nearly an hour later that Rafael returned again and this time some of the tension had gone.

'He *is* all right,' he told Abbie. 'I spoke to him and I spoke with his doctors. It was a small heart attack and he got to the hospital in good time. He's had several stents put in, which has probably saved him from having a much worse attack. Saved his life even...'

As before, Rafael had gone straight to Ella's bedside and was touching her again. A soft touch. And this time it was accompanied by the hint of a smile. Was he trying to transfer the hope from the news about his father to his daughter? Hoping against hope that another life was about to be saved?

Oddly, it made Abbie feel more isolated. She was relieved for Rafael and his family, of course she was, but did this end justify the means? Make it acceptable to put up those emotional barriers when things got tough?

'I…might go and have a shower,' she said. 'And see if I can get a couple of hours' sleep. If you're okay to stay with Ella?'

'Of course.' This time it was Abbie who received that gentle touch. 'I'm here. You do whatever it is you need to do.'

They couldn't spend every minute of every day in that small isolation room with Ella, no matter how hard it was to be away from her.

They had to eat. They had to use the bathroom. They had professional obligations that became more of an issue as the hours ticked into the third day of this crisis, even though their colleagues were only too happy to be covering for them.

'The MacDonalds want to speak to us before Angus is discharged,' Rafael said after a phone call. 'Maybe I should go and see them. It would be bad if they caused trouble for the clinic by making another complaint.'

'I'm sure Ethan could handle it.' But Abbie glanced at a message on her own pager. 'Annabelle's due to have the dressing taken off her new ear today. I do feel bad about missing that.' She tilted her head back to rest on the chair, covering her eyes with her hand. How long could you go on like this? Was there a point where physical and emotional exhaustion simply became too much? What happened then? A numbness that never left? Did you have to go through life like a robot? Going through the motions but incapable of feeling anything, good *or* bad?

'Ella's stable. Maybe it would be a good idea if we had more of a break than we've been getting. As long as one of us is here with her. We don't know how long this is going to go on for.'

Or how it was going to end. Ella was clearly

fighting hard for life because the holding pattern was continuing and she wasn't getting any worse. But they all knew that she could reach the limit of her physical resources at any time. That she could crash and there would be nothing that any of them could do to keep supporting her.

Abbie took her hand from her eyes to find Rafael's concerned gaze resting on her. He wanted to help, didn't he? He just didn't know how because he was too far away. Emotionally distant. Protecting himself.

This was no time to attack him for something he probably couldn't help. Or change. And yet this was the kernel of why their marriage had got into trouble. The part of each other that they didn't get. Abbie thought she could understand why Rafael was like he was now but the real question still remained. Was he capable of giving her what she needed for the rest of her life?

Maybe nobody could. Maybe her expectations were simply too high.

The whole issue of their relationship was too

much for her exhausted mind and body. Yes. Maybe they did need a break from being in here with Ella.

Maybe they needed a break from being with each other.

'You go and see the MacDonalds.' It wasn't as though it would be a new experience to be keeping this kind of a vigil by herself. 'I'll decide later about Annabelle.'

But Rafael was reluctant to go. 'Are you sure? I want to be here for you this time. For every minute.'

Didn't he want to be here for *Ella*? Had he given up hope on her again? Abbie had to blink back tears. She was being irrational but it was hard not to be when you felt this fragile. She had to get a grip. For Ella's sake as well as her own. She couldn't help her precious child if she fell apart herself.

'Go,' she said. 'You'll be back here soon enough. I'll be okay.'

Except she wasn't. Even if Rafael was holding

himself distant emotionally, his presence had been more comforting than she'd realised. Being the only parent with nothing to do but watch and hold the tiny hand that emerged from the bandages covering the tubes was so lonely. So heartbreaking.

Maybe that was why Abbie allowed herself to be persuaded to take a break herself when Rafael came back with the news that a very happy MacDonald family was on its way home.

Her registrar and the ward nurse were surprised to see her appear in the treatment room.

'We weren't expecting you.'

'I needed a break,' Abbie told her colleagues quietly. There was no need for her patient's family to know that she had personal issues that outweighed any professional responsibilities. They were here with *their* precious child. The world outside Ella's room was continuing to revolve and maybe it was a good thing to be reminded of that.

'How's it going?' her registrar asked.

'As well as it can. No change yet.' Abbie raised her voice, turning to the nurse, who was carefully melting the sticky side of tape with an alcohol-dampened cotton bud. 'How's it going *here*?'

It was a fiddly business, removing the elaborate dressing that had been protecting Annabelle's new ear since her surgery. The plastic cup had been taped to her face and bandaged in place. Inside the cup were layers of soft dressings around and inside the ear.

'You're being very brave,' Abbie told her small patient. 'I know it's a bit sore when things stick like this.'

'Can I see it?' Annabelle asked. 'Can I see my new ear?'

'You sure can. It's going to look a bit pink and funny for a while, though. It takes time for the swelling to go down.'

'I want to see it.'

Abbie took a hand mirror from the nurse and held it for Annabelle, who tilted her head and stared intently at her image. The smile that lit up her face moments later was heart-warming.

'Do you like it?'

Annabelle nodded happily. 'I've got *two* earrings.'

'We'll have to put a new big dressing on it and hide it away for another couple of weeks but it's looking great.' Abbie smiled at Annabelle's mother. 'I'm really happy with the result.'

'Oh, so are we, Mrs de Luca. Thank you *so* much.'

It had been a good idea to take the short break. To connect with the world beyond what was happening to Ella. The warmth of Annabelle's smile stayed with Abbie as she hurried back, feeling stronger than she had when she'd left.

The smile with which Rafael greeted her return was also heart-warming. He was beside Ella, stroking her wispy, dark curls and talking to her quietly as a nurse took a set of vital-sign recordings. Abbie waited until the nurse was finished before going close enough to press a kiss to Ella's forehead.

'Hey, baby girl. How are you doing?'

'Still no better,' Rafael said quietly. 'But no worse either. We can only wait. How was Annabelle? Are you happy with the ear?'

Abbie nodded but she didn't want to talk about it. Already, the outside world had vanished again and the only thing that mattered was here in this room. She watched Ella breathing for a minute. Touched her hand that lay upturned, with the fingers curled in complete relaxation, as though she was having a natural sleep.

But this was anything but natural. This was state-of-the-art technology and a battery of medication that was keeping her baby alive. Needing comfort, Abbie picked up Ears. She turned away as she cuddled the toy under her chin. She could smell Ella on the toy and it made her want to cry.

'What's that?'

The fat file open on the chair Rafael had been sitting on distracted her.

'I've been reading Ella's story,' he told Abbie. 'From the first admission. I'd forgotten that we thought she'd just had a cold.'

Abbie sat down and picked up the file. The paediatrician had made meticulous notes.

'"Presenting symptoms,"' she read aloud, '"pale skin, unexplained fever, refusing feeds, crying a lot, irritable..."' Her voice caught. '"Query persistent pain."'

'She was only a few weeks old. Life is so unfair sometimes.'

Abbie was looking at the first sheaf of blood-test results that had come back on Ella. At notes from the new specialists that had been called in. At the plans for chemotherapy, steroid treatment and blood transfusions. The words blurred in front of her.

'It was unbelievable, wasn't it?'

'I thought it was my fault.' Rafael's soft words were shocking.

'What?' Abbie's jaw dropped. 'How could you possibly think that?'

'Because of Freddie.'

'Who's Freddie?' Abbie was bewildered. She'd said that they didn't really know each other but it had never smacked her in the face quite like this. She could see now that Rafael distanced himself as a form of protection but was it so effective she'd never even guessed at something so dark?

Rafael thought that Ella's illness was *his* fault?

'Freddie was a little boy who had ALL.' Rafael was still stroking Ella's head as he spoke softly. A slow, gentle movement of his hand that was probably comforting him as much as Ella, if she was aware of it. 'I got involved in his case just before I left oncology. He was the grandson of some of my parents' closest friends and they insisted that they brought Freddie to me. That, if anyone could save him, I could.' He glanced up at Abbie, one corner of his mouth lifting in a lopsided smile. And then he moved away from Ella, coming to perch one hip on the arm of the chair Abbie was sitting in. 'He was such a sunny child. His parents adored him and would have gone to the ends of the earth to save him.'

As they themselves would have for Ella. As they still would. Abbie swallowed hard.

'The initial treatment went well. He was a good candidate for bone-marrow transplant and, being Italian, of course there were any number of family members who were desperate to get tested. Unfortunately the only match was his little sister, who was only two and she couldn't understand why people wanted to hurt her. It was very tough on the whole family.'

There was more to this story. The absolute faith everybody had in him must have created an unprecedented pressure on Rafael to save this child. Abbie touched Rafael's hand to encourage him to continue.

'The early results after the transplant looked good but Freddie developed graft-versus-host disease. We tried everything we could. I pushed for us to try anything new that had even the slightest hope of success. I persuaded his parents to sign consent forms and told them that the extra suffering would be worth it when we succeeded. I was so determined to save him. And they were desperate to believe in me. I think we all believed that it would work in the end but he was admitted to Intensive Care a few weeks later. He was in there for four weeks. One by one, his vital organs gave up the struggle until there was nothing keeping him alive except for the machines, so there was a meeting and…and they decided it was time to stop. To turn the machines off.'

Abbie felt an icy chill run down her spine. 'You were *there*?'

'No. I was in my office later that day when Freddie's father came to see me. He was distraught. They'd all been through so much. He couldn't believe it hadn't worked. He kept asking me, *"Why…?"* And he was crying. I've never seen a man cry like that. And the way he was looking at me. They had believed in me. They had put their precious little boy through so much pain and suffering because I had persuaded them. And I'd let them down. Failed them all. It ripped me to pieces.'

Abbie squeezed his hand. 'Of course it did.'

'And that was when I decided I couldn't stay in oncology. That it would destroy me in the end. I was a coward and that was why I thought that maybe it was my fault that Ella became ill with cancer. A fitting punishment for my cowardice.'

For a man as proud as Rafael the admission was so huge it took Abbie's breath away.

'I wish you'd told me.'

'And shown my weakness? At a point when you needed me to be strong? What difference could it have made?'

'All the difference in the world,' Abbie whispered. 'That's what I meant by not understanding each other. If I'd known, I would have understood why you were so against the treatment in New York. That you couldn't bear to see Ella continuing to suffer. You'd been through it all before, with Freddie. You knew that the extra pain and suffering might be just that. Extra pain that Ella didn't have to endure. That it wasn't because you didn't care enough.'

Rafael swore softly in Italian. 'How could you ever have thought that I didn't care enough?' The words were fierce enough to sound angry.

'You thought your mother didn't care,' she reminded him quietly. 'She didn't let you in, did she? She couldn't show you how she felt after your father's heart attack. Maybe she was blaming herself. Maybe she was remembering all the arguments they'd ever had and decided that was what had caused it all.'

Rafael was silent. Was he seeing the connection? Understanding something of how *she* had felt when he hadn't been able to listen to how she'd felt about Ella's treatment?

Her breath escaped in a half sob. 'You know what the funny thing is?'

'Funny?'

'Funny sad, I mean. Because there was something I didn't tell you then either.' Maybe the inability to share the important things wasn't completely one-sided. Perhaps she had been trying to protect herself as well by holding back. She couldn't do it any more. She *shouldn't* have done it at all.

'What?'

'That I thought it was *my* fault.'

'*Che cosa*? Why?'

Abbie's voice was choked. 'I've always felt guilty, you know? That I survived when Sophie didn't. My parents loved her so much.'

'I'm sure they loved you too.'

'But it was Sophie who was hurting. Her pain that they couldn't bear. I don't think they even saw *my* pain. I was alive, wasn't I? I was the lucky one.'

'Oh…*cara*…' Somehow Rafael had gathered her into his arms and he was holding her.

'I felt like they couldn't stand seeing me still alive because it reminded them of what they'd lost. And I hated it. I must have made life so much harder for them and I wondered later if that was why they broke up. And…and I thought, maybe Ella getting sick was *my* punishment…to show me how hard it had been for them.'

Rafael held her shoulders firmly, pushing her back far enough to see his face clearly.

'It was not your fault that Ella got sick.'

Abbie held his intense gaze. 'It wasn't your fault either. Don't *ever* think that.'

'I couldn't care more. For Ella *or* you. I would give my life to keep either of you safe.'

'I know that now.' There was a new pain in Abbie's chest. Her heart felt like it might break again but for a different reason this time. Because it felt so full of love it was in danger of bursting at the seams. Maybe the pain came from stretching rather than breaking. Hearts could do that, couldn't they?

Maybe there was even room in there for her own parents, too. Maybe, with her new depth of understanding, she would be able to forgive and old wounds could begin to heal. For all of them.

The beeping of the machinery surrounding

Ella was the only sound in the room for a long moment. Somebody from the team caring for their daughter would no doubt be coming into the room at any time to check on things but just for now, they were in a little bubble of time that was just for them.

A moment that had brought them closer than ever.

A louder beeping was issuing some kind of warning. A dropping level of oxygen saturation, perhaps, or an indication that blood pressure was getting too low.

It made Abbie flinch.

'I can't do this, Rafe,' she whispered fiercely. 'Ella might die and I don't think I can live with that.'

'Yes, you can. If you have to, you can… You must.'

The words sounded oddly strangled. Abbie raised her gaze to see tears on Rafael's face. Tears that chased each other in rapid succession to trickle down the sides of that proud nose and follow the deep grooves to collect at the corners of lips that were trembling.

Tears. From the man who never cried. From the man she'd thought was keeping a safe emotional distance from what was happening to their daughter. A safe distance from her.

Tears from the man she loved so much.

'You can feel that pain and you *can* survive,' Rafael told her brokenly. 'And you know how?'

Abbie shook her head.

'Because you're loved. I'm not like your parents, Abbie. I see your pain. I understand. And… and I *love* you.'

'I love you, too.'

Rafael nodded. 'I know this. And that's how I know I would survive, too. But only if I have you. You only feel afraid if you're not safe and… and maybe I've never been brave enough to let myself feel it, but—'

'We can love each other,' Abbie finished for him. 'We can keep each other safe.'

And, with Rafael's arms tightly around her,

Abbie buried her face against his shoulder for a moment, to gather her strength as people rushed into the room to find out what had tripped the alarm they'd seen from the central station.

'She's fighting the ventilation,' one of them decided. 'Trying to breathe for herself.'

'Maybe it's time we lightened the sedation. How's everything else looking?'

Abbie stood there in the circle of Rafael's arms as the medical team did a thorough assessment on Ella and debated the juggling of her medications and interventions.

She was a fighter, all right, their little daughter.

And they would be here, together. By her side for every minute of this fight.

And whether it ended in victory or not, they would still be together. Abbie knew that now with absolute certainty.

Their marriage had been put through a trial by fire because of Ella's illness. The battle for their little girl's survival wasn't over yet but the reason they'd been pushed apart was.

There was nothing they couldn't survive from now on.

As long as they were together.

Loving each other.

Keeping each other safe.

EPILOGUE

Six months later...

IT WAS EARLY autumn but it still felt like summer here on the Amalfi Coast.

Abbie thought the small Italian town of Amalfi was every bit as beautiful as Rafael had hoped she would.

The perfect place for a wedding.

A place that filled such a special part of his heart. The ancient, sun-baked buildings in soft pastels and terracotta that clung to the foothills of the dramatic cliffs and jostled for space all the way down to the shoreline, where the beach umbrellas took over. The somnolent serenity of the lemon groves high on the hillsides that surrounded his family estate. Rafael was enjoying the view of the lemon groves at the moment, leaning on the warm stone balustrade of the terrace. Taking a moment from a busy day to count his blessings.

Like the warmth and generosity of his family as they were finally able to welcome Abbie and Ella into their midst.

They had been puzzled by the news that Abbie's parents weren't coming to the wedding.

'But why not?'

'It was too far for them to come.'

Abbie hadn't been talking about physical distance. The emotional gap was still too big to bridge but at least the invitation had been offered. Contact had been reestablished and the door was open again. Abbie was quietly confident that, one day, those old wounds would be healed.

'We're going to visit them when we get back to England. They want to see all the photographs.'

The planned visit might have been tentatively suggested and warily accepted but it would be a huge step forward and, in the meantime, Rafael's family was more than prepared to step forward.

'We are your family now, too,' Rafael's father, Georgio, declared, 'and if you will permit me the honour, I will be the one to give this beautiful bride's hand in marriage to my son.'

'It's me who would be honoured,' Abbie had responded. *'Grazie mille, Papa.'*

Oh, they'd loved hearing her not only try out her Italian but take her place in the family. Rafael could understand the tears of joy in his father's eyes because he'd had that reaction himself the first time Ella had called him *Papa*.

She could do more than that now. She could say, *'Ti amo, Papy.'*

I love you, Daddy.

There had been many tears of joy being shed in this part of Salerno over these last few days. His mother and his sister, Marcella, who was going to be Abbie's bridesmaid, were probably encountering a fair few of them today as they took Abbie and Ella out for some last-minute, pre-wedding shopping and probably a gelato down at the beach.

Everyone they met would know the de Luca family and would have heard their story. They would know instantly who the beautiful little toddler was and Mama would no doubt be only too happy to stop and let them marvel.

'Isn't she the *bambina* who has been so terribly ill?'

'But she looks so *sana* now. So healthy…so happy…'

'It's surely *un miracolo*.'

It was indeed *un miracolo*.

The road hadn't been easy but Ella had kept fighting after the life support of the ventilator had been deemed unnecessary and she had gone from strength to strength since then. They'd had another visit back to the hospital when she'd been due for another bone-marrow biopsy at the six-month mark after her ground-breaking treatment and that had gone without any complications. And they'd been rewarded with the same astonishingly good news that they'd had after her last biopsy.

There was no sign of the cancer that had threatened to take this joy from their lives and the new cells were still there, ready to fight any attempted recurrence. It wasn't just the exuberant Italians who were labelling it a miracle. Ella's case was being written up in many journals. Being held up as an example of why all the time and effort and money spent on medical research was worthwhile.

She'd been able to go home the same day that time. Back to their home that was finally a *real* home. One that had a sparkly pink bedroom that Ella adored. He and Abbie had finally managed to paint the silver stars on the ceiling. They'd even managed to stick the glitter on so that they sparkled as much as dancing bear's tutu did. Seeing those stars for the first time had been when they'd heard something they'd never thought they'd hear again.

Ella gurgling with happiness as she'd stretched

her arms and tried to reach the new sparkles in her life.

He and Abbie had looked at each other. They'd both opened their mouths to say it…

Ella's being a plughole…

But neither of them had been able to utter a word because the moment had been so choked by joy.

Just the memory of that moment, the echo of the sound of childish delight, would always melt his heart.

And beneath those stars Ella had a real bed now. There was room for dancing bear and Ears and all sorts of other beloved toys to share her sleeping space.

Her hair had grown back into a soft cluster of dark curls. She was still a little too thin for her age, which made her eyes look even bigger, but she was, without doubt, the most beautiful child that had ever existed.

Being healthy was what really mattered, though.

And his father, busy at the moment searching for the tie that matched his best suit, was also healthy again. Healthier than he had been for many years.

The heart attack had been a blessing in disguise.

Not just because his father had had his damaged arteries repaired and had now modified his lifestyle to exclude smoking and include exercise and would probably live to be Ella's *nonno* for many years to come.

No. The blessing had also come from how shocking his mother's apparent lack of concern had been. How he could see so clearly the damage that emotional distance could inflict on others.

He would never be like that again. Or if it happened even a little before he noticed it, Abbie would remind him. She would only need to look at him with that special look she had for him alone and he would remember how safe he was.

How safe he would always be.

Because Abbie loved him so much.

Rafael de Luca took a deep, deep breath of the warm, lemon-scented air and then straightened and turned to go back inside. Not that he really needed to help with the preparations for the big day tomorrow because it seemed like the whole town had been given a part to play, but he wanted to be part of it. He wanted to revel in every single moment of this special trip home.

He paused for just a heartbeat longer, however, as he let his breath out in a long, contented sigh.

He really was the luckiest man on earth.

Abbie took a deep, deep breath as she got out of the car.

This was it. The long-awaited dream wedding that had been put on hold for so long.

She had known it would be special, coming to Rafael's home town to pledge their commitment to each other in public, but she'd had no idea that she would be so unquestioningly adopted by an entire family.

By a whole town, it seemed.

There were people clapping and cheering already, as Georgio de Luca came to open the door of the car, even though they had a short walk before they got anywhere near the intimidating flight of stone steps that led up to Amalfi's famous ninth-century cathedral. Cars couldn't get into the narrow streets that led to the *piazzo*.

The soft fabric of her wedding dress rippled around her as she got out of the car into the warmth of an endless Italian summer afternoon. Abbie had wanted traditional but not over the top and her classic lace dress had a fitted, beaded bodice, a tiny waist and a deliciously swirly, feminine skirt that brushed the ground and had just a small train.

She'd chosen a natural style for her hair, too, because she knew Rafael loved it best when it was loose and flowing. The hairdresser had tamed the waves into shapely, soft curls, clipped some of the hair back to keep it out of her face and then cleverly looped some of the tresses to create a casually elegant look that was perfect for the tiny white flowers that would be her only accessories. It had seemed too much to hope for that lemon blossoms would be available so early in the season but somehow it had been made possible.

Abbie hadn't wanted a veil and as she stepped out to see the blue sparkle of the sea and the happy faces of people lining the route she was about to take into the Piazzo del Duomo, she knew she'd made the right decision. She didn't want anything that would put even a flimsy barrier in front of any part of this day.

Smiling her thanks at Georgio, Abbie turned and bent down to peer into the car.

'You ready, baby girl?'

A mop of shiny, dark curls adorned with a clip that held a tiny lemon blossom flower to match the ones in Abbie's hair nodded agreement but Ella didn't wait for her mother's help. She wriggled across the seat, turned onto her tummy and slid out of the car.

Her dress was pink, of course. A version of the same tutu that her ballerina bear still wore, and Ella adored it. She loved her lacy white socks too and the sheer cuteness of the pink ballet pumps on her small feet would always make her parents smile.

Marcella was hurrying to catch up from the other side of the car.

'Ella. Come here, *cara*. *Zia* Marcella will carry you to the church.'

'No. Ella *walk*.'

'It's a long way, *cara*.'

Abbie smiled at the new sister she already loved. 'Let her walk, Marcella. Her little legs will get tired before we get halfway up those steps and then we can pick her up.'

It wasn't Ella's legs getting tired so much as the press of people wanting to see the arrival of the bride that made her want to be carried. And it wasn't her new aunty that she wanted.

'Mum-mum-mum...'

Abbie handed her bouquet to Marcella to carry and scooped Ella into her arms.

'It's a long way,' Marcella said anxiously. 'Maybe Papa should carry her?'

Abbie looked at the huge set of steps she needed to carry her daughter up. It would be a challenge but nothing compared to the challenges they had already faced and won. Smiling, she declined the offer.

Somewhere, at the top of all those stairs, Rafael was waiting for them. The love of her life.

Ella's papa.

How perfect was it that she would carry their daughter into the ceremony that would show the world their commitment to each other as a family?

She shifted Ella into a slightly more secure position on one hip as Marcella arranged her train so that it would flow beautifully up the steps.

A quick glance down at her dress showed her that nothing was out of place.

Abbie pressed a quick kiss to Ella's curls to hide her smile.

She'd always said she didn't want to be a pregnant bride but this was okay because it was early days.

Still a secret between her and Rafael.

She couldn't wait any longer. Abbie began to climb the steps.

It wasn't really okay, was it?

It was more like *perfect*.

* * * * *